# The Ross Family Adventures

## Whistling Creek

# RACHEL GRACE

The Ross Family Adventures:
*Whistling Creek*
by Rachel Grace

Published by Wendilla Press

Illustrated by Kaelyn Reese.

ISBN: 978-1-7373285-2-0 (print)

Printed in the United States of America

First Edition

3

# The Ross Family Adventures

*Whistling Creek*

WENDILLA
PRESS

# CONTENTS

# The Wagon Train

## May 1863

# CHAPTER 1

# The Story of the Blizzard

"Are we there yet?" The monotone hum of the wagon train was broken by five-year-old Anna Ross in the back of their wagon.

Her older brother Joshua looked at her and shook his head, weariness on his face. He already thought their trip was more boring than he expected, and it didn't help to remind him that they had only been on the trail a month. They still had at least another to go. "No, Anna. We only left Independence yesterday."

"But I want to be home now!" Anna said. "I'm tired of living in a wagon!"

"You and me both," Joshua murmured with a deep breath.

Joshua's twin, nine-year-old Sarah, heard her brother's remark from Malachi, the Morgan horse, and sighed. She was riding close enough to the rest of her family so she could still be involved in the wagon conversation, but also far enough away to try to avoid the dust stirred up by the thirty prairie schooners and buggies in their wagon train. The wagons traveled in a straight line, and the Ross children's wagon was near the back. It was as if they were walking through a wall of brown. They ate dust, breathed dust, and sneezed dust. It covered their dishes, and every day when they stopped, the oldest sisters would have to shake out their bedding, creating miniature dust storms. It grew tiresome, the same routine day in and day out, but it was safer in a large band of wagons than alone. Even when the Ross family had traveled on their own, there had been dust, but they had not minded it as much. Eighteen-year-old Rebecca had said, "At least I knew it was our dust and no one else's," when she was found shaking her head in disdain at the mess the previous day. Even her sweet nature was becoming flustered by the muddle.

The train was traveling down the Oregon Trail, but their wagon, as well as two other families, were going to branch off the trail later on to continue on their own path to Colorado Territory. Sarah smiled at how far her family had come in the past three months. The year 1863 had started full of hope for the eight Ross children and their parents. They'd had grand plans of moving west to start a new life together. But then February hit, and the Ross siblings' world was thrown into disarray. Their parents, Joseph and Martha, caught the terrible disease smallpox, and both passed away. The siblings continued to live on their family's farm in their small town of Augusta, Missouri, but two months after their parents' deaths, the oldest siblings, Rebecca and Reuben, decided to follow Pa's dream to move west. It was anything but easy, but Sarah finally felt satisfied that it was paying off since they were on their way west. Clicking to Malachi, Sarah pulled on the reins to the left. Growing farther away from the wagon would mean she couldn't talk with the rest of her siblings, but it also meant she would be able to breathe without choking.

In an attempt at a joke, thirteen-year-old Abraham, who was driving the wagon because his older brother's arm was sprained from a previous accident, announced, "Today, folks, we will see dirt, bugs, and, maybe the most exciting thing of all—lots of dust!" He chuckled to himself, and as he did so, Rebecca, who was sitting next to him on the wagon seat, shook her head with a grin. His jest rang with truth. The prairie stretched out before them, barren and stark, with no beauty to be found.

Rebecca sighed and ran her finger along the side of the seat. It was a never-ending wasteland that they were crossing. She shut her eyes to imagine their farm back in Missouri. Trees, beautiful and wisping. Mountains, tall and magnificent, rising out of the ground. Thunder rolling off them in the far-off distance. Friendly squirrels in the branches of apple trees and coyotes hunting the gophers in the night. She sighed. She missed home dearly. *Will we ever find another like it?* she wondered.

"Are we going to stop to make camp soon?" Emily asked quietly from the bed in the wagon, her brown eyes shining. At a full year older than Anna, she was more soft-spoken and tended to get into less trouble than her rambunctious sister.

"Um . . ." Abraham paused, then looked back at

his older brother, who sat on one of the Rosses' beds. "Reuben?"

The sixteen-year-old shrugged his shoulders. "I don't know, Abe. Maybe another hour or so. We may travel longer than usual today because of those storm clouds in the distance. I was talking with Josie Sellers's pa, and he and some of the other men think we might get a large thunderstorm tonight. There's a possibility, from Mr. Sellers's point of view at least, that there may be some hail in it."

"A hailstorm?" Rebecca repeated in disbelief. She shifted around to gaze at him with a raised eyebrow. "In early May? You've got to be joking!"

Reuben shook his head. "No, I'm not. Mr. Sellers said they sometimes happen out here. From what I understand, they're unpredictable and can show up out of nowhere. Now, don't ask me how he got that idea, but I don't want to take a chance."

"At least we're out of blizzard season," Joshua

mumbled, lying down on the bed he'd been sitting on.

Anna shivered, overhearing him. "I don't like hailstorms, and I definitely don't like blizzards."

Reuben looked down at her in compassion. "Neither do I, Anna. At least we don't have to worry about blizzards on this trip. You know, I almost died in a blizzard back in Missouri."

The three children in the back of the wagon gaped at him. Rebecca hid her grin from the rest of her siblings and looked at Abraham out of the corner of her eye. He also had a smile building on his face, and Rebecca knew he remembered. She subtly put her finger to her lips, signaling for him not to ruin the tale. He nodded and tried to keep a straight expression.

"For real?" Joshua inquired.

"You're joking, right?" Anna added, her eyebrow raised suspiciously. She crossed her arms and tried her best to look like Rebecca did when she scolded her for doing something naughty.

Reuben's brown eyes twinkled, the way Pa's used to right before he told a story. Emily noticed it and squealed. "Tell us the story!" she begged. "Tell us the story!"

"All right, Emily, all right," Reuben agreed, chuckling quietly as he patted his sister's head. "Just let me check on Susan and Sarah. I don't like having them riding too close to the wagons, in case Star or Malachi should buck. I don't want them getting hurt." Reuben leaned out the back of the wagon and shouted to Susan and Sarah, "You girls okay back there?"

Fifteen-year-old Susan yelled back, "All good on our end! Just extremely dusty!"

Reuben nodded in satisfaction, then turned to his younger siblings in the wagon. He tapped his head thoughtfully. "So, the story of how I almost died in a blizzard. Now, how did that go again? I believe I have suddenly forgotten. Dear me, I guess you'll never know. What a shame."

Anna groaned and jumped into Reuben's lap. "You're being silly!" She shook her finger at him.

Reuben grabbed Anna's wrist with his good hand and pretended to bite her finger. "You know, that's pretty good!" he teased.

Anna squealed and pulled her hand away, giggling.

Reuben laughed, rubbing his stomach like he'd just finished a great dinner. "You know me all too well, Miss Anna! Well, here's how our story begins. It was a dark and snowy night in the deep—"

"That's the oldest beginning in the books!" Joshua criticized, shaking his head.

Reuben grinned and wiped at his mouth. "No, truly, Joshua, that's how it began. During the winter when I was twelve years old, a huge blizzard came up out of nowhere. It lasted for hours, and I thought it would *never* end. It was cold and dark, and the only place warm enough was right by the kitchen stove. That meant we couldn't do anything at all besides sit and talk. I must admit that as a little kid I was very impatient, something I had to deal with the hard way. I'm afraid I made poor Ma quite miserable as I asked endless questions and complained about having to sit still. It wasn't her fault a blizzard had come up, and I should have known that. Unfortunately, I was about to learn a hard lesson. After about six hours, I became so restless that I said, 'Ma, I'm going to go do the chores, and no blizzard is going to stop me!' Ma begged me to wait until Pa came back from town and the blizzard stopped, but I was stubborn and refused to listen to reason. I pulled on my big boots and my thick buffalo coat and tromped out into the snow, carrying a lantern so I could at least see two inches in front of my face.

I knew that if I just walked in a straight line I'd hit the side of the barn, and then would be able to feel my way to the door. Well, that plan worked well getting to the barn, and I was able to take care of the animals—now, this was before we had Bessie and the draft horses of course, so only Malachi, Star, and our old cow, Rosie, were there—but coming out and starting to walk back to the house, I realized I didn't know which way the house was!"

He said it in such a comical way that Joshua, Emily, and Anna had to laugh, though they were hanging on to his every word, the suspense too much for them to take. Reuben paused a moment, then continued. "I decided that the best plan now was to simply turn around and walk back to the barn and warm up against Star or Malachi until the storm was over. At least I wouldn't freeze to death then. Somehow, though, I must have not turned around enough, and I walked for what seemed like forever without touching the barn. I started to panic and began to call out for help. Everything was white and gray and cold, and the lantern went out. I couldn't see anything. The snow was swirling around me, and the wind bit my face. I knew I was going to die. Next thing I remember is Abraham shaking me in our bed up in the loft and saying, 'Reuben! Stop it! Quit yelling; you're waking everyone up!' I sat up and looked around; everyone was staring at me like I was crazy, and Emily, you were just a little thing, and you were bawling. I didn't understand for a moment; I thought I had somehow been rescued. Then everything made sense. I'd been having a nightmare!"

Joshua, Emily, and Anna exploded, laughing so hard that tears ran down their faces. Up on the wagon seat, Rebecca was silently shaking, holding her hand to her mouth, and Abraham was doubled over, trying to catch his breath from the memory of it. Reuben sat with a grin on his face that was both amused and embarrassed.

"I still remember the look on your face when you realized . . ." Abraham couldn't finish his sentence. He threw up his hands and slapped his knee with another roar of laughter. "It was priceless!"

Reuben shrugged and waved it off, shaking his head, cheeks red but smiling. "Priceless—or the biggest embarrassment of my life. I'll argue the latter to my death."

"I'd say it was a mix of both," Rebecca said with a giggle.

"You've *got* to tell that story to Sarah and Susan tonight when we stop!" Emily insisted once she was able to talk again.

"I'm sure Susan remembers," Reuben replied, "as it's not an easy thing to forget—it was certainly not one of my proudest moments. But I'll make sure to tell Sarah. She was Anna's age at the time, so I don't know if she remembers it."

"Well, we were the same age, and I didn't remember it, so I bet she won't either," Joshua said.

"I'd remember something that funny," Anna objected, hands on hips.

Reuben pulled one of his little sister's curly ringlets. "I'm sure you would, Anna Banana."

"I'm going to tell that story to Michael and Micah," Joshua added. Even though they'd only met three days earlier, Joshua was already great friends with Michael and Micah Sellers, who were a year younger than he was. He could already picture their hilarious reactions when they heard the tale.

Reuben's face contorted with a mix of dread and enjoyment at the thought of his story traveling beyond their wagon. He debated banning the tale from being spread, but then he shrugged. It wasn't that big of a deal.

"And I'm going to tell it to Ida!" Emily declared.

Ida was Michael and Micah's younger sister, and Emily's new favorite friend.

After a couple more hours of riding in the tight, dusty wagon, the wagon train stopped and made camp. The way they set up their camp was unique, and all for safety. All the wagons parked in a giant circle, and in the middle of the circle, fires were built on which to cook suppers, and tents were set up. The camp echoed with the hubbub of over fifty children and forty adults, all going in different directions. Unless they had to, no one ventured outside the circle. It felt secure in the middle of the wagons, especially as night fell and the surroundings grew a dismal black. Even the animals were kept inside the ring to protect against cattle rustlers and horse thieves.

As soon as the wagons pulled to a halt, the four youngest Ross siblings—Anna, Emily, Joshua, and Sarah—raced to find their friends. Joshua met up with Micah and Michael by their tent, and Jack Donner joined them. Six-year-old Ida Sellers joined in a game of Double Dutch jump rope along with Emily, Sarah, and another nine-year-old girl named Amelia Grant. There was one difference to Amelia jumping Double Dutch than all the other girls. She was blind. She had caught a fever when she was four, leaving her permanently without her sight. It was amazing to watch Amelia jump Double Dutch. She was the best out of all the little girls in the wagon train, and she did it all by listening to the rhythm of the ropes hitting the ground.

Ida and Sarah whirled the ropes as Emily and Amelia jumped hand in hand, chanting the rhyme they had made up the day before. "Wagon train, wagon train, up and down, all this dust makes me frown! We'll be home without a care, how many miles till we get there? One mile, two miles, three miles, four miles . . ."

They made it all the way up to nine before Emily tripped. Amelia fell in a heap on top of her but quickly picked herself back up. The girls burst into giggles as they set to work untangling the ropes, and once they were done, they started the rhyme all over again, this time with Sarah and Ida in the middle.

# CHAPTER 2

# Trouble in
# the Train

It was near twilight. Suppers had already been
cooked and eaten, and now the women were
working on cleaning up the messes while the
younger children joined their friends so they could
play in what little light they had left. The men and
older children tended to livestock and tied dogs
to wagon wheels. Rebecca and her cousin Lydia
sang as they washed the two families' dishes over
a heated pot of water. Susan's soft voice joined the
melody as she dried the clean dishes and set them

into crates. Reuben took care to make sure all their animals were accounted for and tied tightly to the wagon to keep them from wandering off. He wished they had a dog with them. Dogs were wonderful lookouts because they would bark and growl to alert if someone was tampering with their owner's livestock. The Ross family had had a faithful collie named Pepper up until a year before, when she died after saving Anna from a deadly snake. She had been a sweet companion and a strong protector. If she had not taken the bite for Anna, the youngest Ross sibling would likely not be playing a wild game of hide-and-seek with her friends in the wagon train. Reuben missed their friend. Pepper had been around for almost longer than he could remember. With a sigh, he ducked under the wagon with a tool in his hand to tighten the wagon's front left wheel. It had been sounding loose the final mile of their journey that day.

"Got a problem, Reuben?" A voice made him jump and hit his head on the belly of the wagon. He groaned and rubbed his skull as a boy leaned under and smiled a greeting.

"Andy," Reuben grumbled, sliding himself out from the wagon, "maybe save the friendly question until I'm not lying on my back under a low object."

"Oh, yeah, sorry about that." Andy grinned and offered his hand to Reuben, then dragged him to his feet. He inspected the wheel which still had the tool jammed through the center of it. "Your wheel giving you some trouble?"

"Yes." Reuben scratched his head and shrugged. "I'm trying to figure out why it's wobbling. I don't want it coming off while we're traveling. I've already greased it."

"Hmm. You've checked the spokes?"

Reuben shook his head and gave the wheel a nudge with the toe of his boot. None of the spokes moved. Andy frowned and squatted down to examine it. He was also a sixteen-year-old orphan who had lost his father to a logging accident back in Louisiana, and his mother had passed from an unknown sickness the year after, when he was fourteen. He had then hired himself as a ranch hand to the Park family and was moving west with them. He took a deep breath beside the wheel and ran his hands over the spokes.

"Maybe it's a bolt," Andy finally said as Reuben knelt beside him. "I think this one's a hair loose. Might be faulty or something. It's nothing serious, I don't believe. This is a sturdily built wagon." He tapped a pin, then stood. "Let me run and get Mr. Park. He may be able to fix your problem."

"Thanks, Andy."

The sun began to set. Abraham was chatting with Josie Sellers, who was thirteen like he was, and her brother Christopher when he felt something cold and wet land on his nose.

"What in the world?" he whispered, pushing back his hat and looking up at the sky. It was starting to rain.

"I don't like the looks of all those clouds," eleven-year-old Christopher said as a cold wind whipped through the camp. Josie's skirt billowed, and Abraham held on to his hat so he didn't lose it.

Abraham looked around. Others were murmuring about the coming storm as well. Just then, a bolt of lightning lit up the sky. People were starting to run into tents and wagons for shelter as the skies opened with a vengeance and more lightning struck the ground close to the camp.

"We should get back to our folks," Josie yelled over the roaring torrents and shouting families in the

*The skies opened with a vengeance.*

mad rush to get out of the storm. "We don't want to be caught out here and catch a cold or something." A jagged finger of lightning danced across the sky, and Josie screeched. "Or get hit by lightning, for that matter! Come on, Christopher!"

"Yeah, I should get back to my family's wagon as well," Abraham agreed loudly. "Good night, you two! Stay dry!"

"You do the same, Abraham! See you tomorrow morning." Josie grinned and held her hands over her head in an effort to keep the rain off.

Josie and Christopher splashed through some puddles that were already gathering as they ran to their wagon. Abraham waved, then went back to his wagon as fast as possible. The rest of the siblings were already inside, and Anna was complaining and squirming as Rebecca attempted to dry her hair with a towel. Rebecca, in her calm and soothing way, rubbed her little sister dry despite Anna's protests.

Susan pushed a stray blond whisp of hair back into her chignon, a low bun at the nape of the neck, before saying, "Hey, boys, I was thinking, maybe you shouldn't sleep under the wagon tonight. It will be far too wet under there with the way the rain's falling. Ugh, it's practically sideways."

"I was thinking the same as Susan," Rebecca agreed, nodding. "There's no need to have you poor boys get soaked just so we can have a little more space up here. It'll be tighter than usual, but we'll survive. Joshua, you can sleep in with the little girls, and Reuben and Abe . . . well, maybe you'll have to sleep sitting up."

"That's okay. I won't freeze or anything." Abraham shifted from his perch on a barrel lid and wrapped his arms around himself, acting like a pitiful puppy trying to keep warm. Something soft hit his face, and he pulled it off to find a towel in his hand and a smirk on Rebecca's face. He chuckled.

Outside, the wind howled like a pitiful dog, and it shook the little wagon. The rain made quite a racket as it hit the canvas, and there was hardly any way to keep it from getting inside because of the wind whipping it in every direction possible. Rebecca and Reuben worked to close up the entry flaps at the back and front of the wagon. They leaned out into the rain and tried desperately to grab the pieces of canvas, a difficult feat to accomplish when the wind was so strong. Reuben reached out, stretching himself to the max, and his good hand connected with the flap. He slid back inside and onto Susan and Rebecca's bed, still holding onto the canvas. As he secured it to the wagon seat, Rebecca caught the other flap and brought it down as well. Reuben quickly sealed them up, and they did the same thing at the back of the wagon. Afterward, Rebecca took her hair down and dried it with a towel, then tossed the towel to Reuben.

"Phew!" he exclaimed, wiping off his face. "It sure is nasty out, isn't it?"

"Will we be okay, Reuben?" Emily asked, her face scrunched up in worry. She shivered, still damp from being caught out in the downpour.

"I sure hope so, Em," he replied, rubbing her shoulders. "It shouldn't be as bad as the last storm we had in the wagon. Though . . . it's getting strangely colder. I wonder if we *are* in for some hail."

The temperature continued to drop steadily the rest of the night as more and more rain fell. The siblings spent the night huddled together under quilts and buffalo robes to keep warm. No one slept, because it was simply too cold, too wet, and too loud. The wagon canvas could only sustain a certain amount of rain, and soon it didn't even seem to make a difference. The siblings cuddled close, and Anna whimpered throughout the night. Hail came at different intervals, hitting the canvas roof of the wagon. Luckily, they were only about the size of a penny and didn't do too much damage to the wagons.

Around dawn, as the rain began to calm, Anna moaned. "I don't feel so good, Becca." She curled up into a little ball on her straw tick mattress.

Rebecca looked at her little sister. "What? What kind of don't feel good? Like, are you sick, or does your stomach hurt, or . . ."

"My stomach," Anna said with a gag. She hid her head in her pillow and moaned.

Rebecca jerked uneasily at the sound. Anna was always a little overly dramatic, but this seemed to be a little too much.

"Mine hurts too, Becca," Emily said, her breath coming out in little clouds as she talked.

Joshua and Sarah also admitted to feeling sick.

Rebecca's eyebrows drew into a frown as she asked what they felt like. All four of the youngest

siblings complained of a bad stomach ache and
feeling queasy. Rebecca placed the back of her hand
on each of their foreheads. They were all a little
warmer than usual. Rebecca's and Susan's faces both
grew concerned. Sickness on the trail was never a
good thing. But where had they caught it? Had the
children been playing with anyone who seemed sick?
Rebecca asked this question to Joshua.

He nodded and said softly, "We went to the
Grant's wagon yesterday morning. I don't know if
anyone was sick, but we each took a drink out of
their water barrel after playing tag. I'm . . . I'm sorry,
Bec."

Trying to keep her voice steady, Rebecca said,
"No, Joshua, it's all right." She straightened from
her bent-over position on the bed and wiped her
hands on her apron. She shut her eyes for a moment.
*Oh, Ma, how I need you. Who to ask?* Her eyes snapped
open. "Abe, run over to the Sellers's wagon and ask

Mrs. Sellers to come here. Tell her Joshua, Sarah, Emily, and Anna aren't feeling well and I could use her help."

"All right, Rebecca," Abraham replied solemnly, pulling on his big buffalo overcoat. He launched out of the wagon and into the cold, wet outdoors.

Meanwhile, Rebecca and Susan tried to coax their siblings to eat some hardtack while Reuben sat and watched and worried. After a few anxious minutes, Mrs. Sellers and Abraham climbed into the wagon. Mrs. Sellers was wrapped in a shawl, and her motherly eyes were concerned as she looked at Emily, Anna, and the twins.

"I'm praying it's nothing serious," Rebecca said as Mrs. Sellers straightened from bending over Anna in bed.

"I'm doing the same," Mrs. Sellers replied quietly, eyes full of compassion as she took Rebecca's hands in hers. "Look, Rebecca, we have two wagons.

Let's move Joshua, Sarah, Emily, and Anna into our extra wagon. My family sleeps in our main wagon and in the tent. The extra wagon we use strictly for supplies. Really, let's move them. That way, I can help you take care of them, and you children will have a better chance of not catching it."

"You don't have to do this," Rebecca insisted, putting a wet cloth on Emily's forehead.

"Yes, I do, Rebecca. I'm sure your ma would have done the same thing for us if we were in this situation. I'm going to get Timothy to help us move them." With that, Mrs. Sellers climbed out of the wagon and walked to hers to get her husband. Rebecca chewed on her lip, trying not to think the worst. She had to be strong; the others expected her to be. If she wasn't, she knew it would scare them. She whispered a prayer and took a deep breath. When she looked up, Reuben's head was also bent, and his lips were moving. Rebecca clasped Susan's hand and sat down on their bed wearily. If only Ma was here. She would know what to do. She would not be scared. Tears slipped down Rebecca's cheeks as she almost felt her mother's reassuring arm around her. It was in times like this that Rebecca missed her mother the most. Suddenly, she realized there *was* an arm around her. Rebecca opened her eyes and found Susan squeezing her tightly. Rebecca let slip a tiny smile.

"Thanks, Su," she whispered, wrapping her arms around her sister.

The four sick Ross siblings had fevers by now. Joshua moaned as quietly as he could, trying to conceal it from Rebecca. Her sharp ears heard him, though, and in an instant she was by his side.

"You're going to be right as rain in a day or so," Rebecca assured her little brother cheerfully, though on the inside she was filled with anxiety. She took a cloth, dipped it in the water bucket on the ground, and placed it on Joshua's forehead.

"Thanks, Bec," he whispered weakly.

She nodded and kissed him on the forehead.

Soon, Mr. and Mrs. Sellers came in, and one by one Mr. Sellers lifted each sick Ross child, wrapped them in a quilt to guard against the cold, and carried them to his wagon. Once inside the other wagon, Mrs. Sellers and Rebecca began the fight to help the siblings recover.

Josie Sellers walked over to the Rosses' wagon and to Reuben and Abraham, who were working on setting up a tent borrowed from a neighbor. Susan and the two of them weren't allowed to go into their wagon for a few days so it would have time to decontaminate from the germs.

Josie's bright smile wasn't as bright as she tried to reassure Abraham, "Your siblings will be all right."

Abraham tried to smile back as he fought with a tent pole. He snapped it into place, then replied, "I hope so. I don't even know where they could have gotten it. I don't even think anyone in the Grant family is sick."

"Oh, they are," Reuben said grimly, grunting as he finished with the tent. "Everyone in the family has it. It's not good, that's for sure."

Abraham got a sinking feeling in his stomach. He sat down in the dewy grass, and when he stood again, his back side was soaked. "Oh, it's wet." He put his hand there, then added, "That's Amelia's family—the blind girl Sarah and Emily are friends with. Is she okay?"

"I'm not sure, Abe."

Abraham tapped his foot on the ground, deep in thought. "What are we going to do? Keep going or wait until they're better?"

"We'll stay here. Some of the wagons are continuing on, and others are going back to town to get help. Our cousins Samuel and Lydia are staying to help, but no one wants to catch whatever this is. Hey, Josie, are you all right?" Reuben stomped a tent peg into the ground and looked at their friend, who was unusually silent.

She gave herself a little shake and attempted a smile. "Yeah . . . yeah. Just worried. Can we pray for everyone who's sick right now?"

"Absolutely," Reuben said, sweeping off his hat and kneeling.

# Joshua's Battle

*You're going to be right as rain in a day or so.* Rebecca's resolute, comforting statement had come back to slap her hard in the face. Five nerve-racking days passed, tireless days and sleepless nights for Mrs. Sellers and Rebecca. They weren't seeing any improvement in any of the siblings. Finally, on days six and seven, to the Ross family's delight, Sarah and Anna gradually grew well and were able to go back into the Rosses' wagon, though they were still very weak. Joshua and Emily, on the other hand, were struggling to improve. In the Grant family, only Mr. Grant was feeling well enough to move about.

Two other families had it, but seemed to have a lighter case than the others. There were nights when Rebecca thought the morning would never arrive. Doctor Preston, the kindly doctor who had helped Reuben back in Independence, rode out to try to help the four sick families, but there wasn't much he could do.

Abraham felt like he was reliving the time when Pa and Ma had been sick with smallpox. He earnestly prayed Joshua and Emily would be a different story. The Sellers were helping the Rosses in any way they could, which reminded him of the way the Wood family had helped them during Ma and Pa's illness. Josie was constantly encouraging Abraham that Joshua and Emily would be okay, though even her encouragement was tinged with anxiety.

Another day passed. Emily made a slow turn in the direction of recovery, but Joshua continued to fight the sickness. Anna was puzzled when she would hear Joshua yell at her to put down a torch when she wasn't even holding one. In fact, she wasn't even in the wagon with him!

"Joshua, I don't have a torch! Why are you talking like that?" Anna said to the wagon canvas.

Susan gently pulled Anna aside and said, "He's talking like that because of the fever, Anna. He doesn't know where he is or what's happening."

"Why?" Anna asked.

"Well, it's just because of the fever. Don't ask me too much; I don't really know why either. He just sees things that aren't there. I've got to go make dinner now. Stay out of the way if you can." Susan hurried away.

Anna looked down at her feet. Susan was under a lot of stress—all her siblings were—and she felt like she just got in everyone's space at the worst times. She knew her brothers and sisters still loved her, but she felt neglected and pushed out her lower lip. With a sob, Anna thought of her ma. Ma would have made sure she was paid attention to. Anna peeked into the wagon where Joshua was, lying in a bed of sweat on a mattress. "Joshua, get better so you can play with me. I miss you."

Joshua groaned in his sleep, and Anna cowered back. Mrs. Sellers, who was coming to take over for Rebecca, saw Anna's fear and held her arms out to her. Anna ran to her, buried her golden head in Mrs. Sellers's skirt, and started to cry.

Mrs. Sellers rubbed Anna's back comfortingly as she whispered, "Oh, Anna, don't cry. We're doing all we can for Joshua. There now, dear. Dry your tears." Her warm, soothing voice, which trilled like a peaceful lullaby on a dark night, reminded Anna of someone she had loved and lost just three months before. In a quiet, trembling voice, she said, "You hug just like my ma."

Mrs. Sellers smiled and hugged Anna tight. Feeling secure for the first time in months, Anna cuddled into Mrs. Sellers and heaved a tiny sigh of contentment.

In the Rosses' tent, Rebecca peeked in to give a report on Joshua. "He's hanging in there," she tried to say brightly. "I don't know what we would have done without Mrs. Sellers. She knows so much more about treating sickness than I do. They are such a wonderful family."

"Yeah, they sure are," Abraham agreed softly.

Susan, Reuben, Sarah, and Emily voiced their agreement.

The next day, as Rebecca wiped her brother's little body down with a cool, wet cloth to try to bring down his temperature, Joshua opened his eyes and whispered in a feeble voice, "Becca? I've been dreaming for so long."

Rebecca started to cry in relief as Joshua

46

attempted a smile. After eight long days, Joshua's fever broke, and he slowly began to eat and drink again. All his siblings were happy beyond words, as were the Sellers family and the Ross siblings' cousins, Samuel and Lydia Willoughby. A few days later Joshua felt good enough to sit up in bed, and a couple days after that, he was laughing again. Once he was able to get out of bed, he took to sitting outside the wagon in the prairie grass, always with a stick and knife in hand. Finally, two weeks after first contracting the sickness, everyone in the wagon train felt good enough to continue west.

Abraham thanked God that all his siblings had survived despite the odds and were now almost back to normal.

# CHAPTER 4

# Reasons and Worries

A week after they had gotten back on the trail, the two oldest Ross girls took time to do the laundry at a small creek they were camping by. They worked mainly in silence, though a tune sometimes passed between them before returning to quiet. Susan suddenly asked Rebecca a startling question.

"Why didn't we contact Uncle Royce and Aunt Amy when Ma and Pa passed away? Wouldn't they have taken us in? And what about Uncle Robert and Aunt Caralee?"

Rebecca looked up, surprised at her sister's remembrance of their mother's brothers and sisters-in-law. They had not seen Uncle Royce and Aunt Amy since they moved from their house in Kentucky seven years earlier. It had been even longer since they'd seen their mother's oldest brother, Robert. She looked down at the pile of clothes she was folding, then glanced away. "Well, we sent a letter to Uncle Robert and Aunt Caralee, telling them what had happened. As for Uncle Royce and Aunt Amy . . . it was foolish of Reuben and me, I know," she whispered softly, "not to tell them what happened. But we wanted to do whatever it took to stay a family, and we were afraid that since Uncle Royce and Aunt Amy have no children, eight new additions all at once would be too much for them. Reuben and I were scared that if we wrote to them, they'd insist on taking us all back to Willoughby Grounds, Ma, Uncle Robert, and Uncle Royce's family mansion."

49

Susan frowned. "Why is that a bad thing?" she asked.

Rebecca bit her lip. "It isn't, but there was a possibility in Reuben's mind that they would send us four oldest to boarding school while they had the little ones adopted into families that wanted to care for them. I agreed." She fidgeted with her hands nervously, then admitted, tears standing out in her eyes, "It was a hard choice to make, one of the hardest in my life so far. But . . . I didn't want to lose any of you. Ma and Pa would give everything for us to stay together. Ma said we needed each other and could never be split up. I know she was right."

Susan wrung her apron in her hands, then said in a tiny voice, "I never want us to be split up."

Rebecca looked over at her sister and smiled, then wrapped an arm around her shoulders. "Neither do I." She paused for a moment before adding, "Look, Su, it was wrong of me to jump to conclusions of how Uncle Royce and Aunt Amy would deal with the situation. Maybe they would have kept us together. It was the fear of the unknown that frightened me and worried Reuben. But I'm learning now—or reminding myself of it—that God directs our steps and will never leave us."

"I'm glad of that." Susan bent over and scrubbed at a shirt on the washboard. "Out in the prairie I feel so—"

"Alone?" Rebecca finished, nodding as she wiped a strand of hair back with a wet hand.

"Yes." Susan laid out the shirt to dry on the large rock next to her, then leaned back on her knees, pulling a briar from her apron.

"Is that why you asked about Uncle Royce and Aunt Amy? Do you want to turn back?"

Susan shrugged, staring at the horizon, nothing but grass ahead. "No . . . and yes. I just wanted to see if we had anything to go back to."

Rebecca considered this for a minute, then clucked her tongue against the roof of her mouth. "Well, the Woods would always take us in if we went back and asked. Do you really, truly want to go back to Augusta? Because you know we all must be in on this; otherwise, we will turn around. That was something we agreed upon when we set out. If one of us wants to go home or feels like this was a bad idea, then we'll turn back."

"But what is home anymore, Becca?" Susan seemed downcast. "We sold the farm to Mr. Wilson."

"What have we here?" Reuben's voice came from behind him, and the sisters looked over their shoulders as he sat down in between them, hands folded over his knees. "Why all the solemn faces? Has one of you turned my white shirt pink again or something? Go ahead and tell me; I can stand the shock—for a second time."

Rebecca and Susan laughed, shaking their heads,

and then Rebecca explained the details of the prior conversation to their brother.

He took a deep breath and rubbed his chin. "You're really considering asking to go back to Augusta, Su?" he questioned, disappointment in his tone. Ever since they had started their adventure over a month earlier, the trip had become as much of Reuben's dream as it had been Pa's. And now he looked devastated that they might have to turn back.

Susan was sobbing. "I don't know! I have been miserable on so many different occasions out here! It's so wide open and large, and we're so small and we really don't have that many in our wagon train. It scares me. Sometimes I think I see shadows outside our wagon train's circle at night. Remember the story we heard about the Oatman family? Yavapai tribe members killed all but three of the nine in the family. Two of the sisters, Olive and Mary Ann, survived, but they were taken captive! I don't want

*"You're really considering asking to go
back to Augusta, Su?"*

that to happen to us. That *can't* happen to us!"

Rebecca nodded, pondering the tale she had heard the year she was eleven. The Oatman family had branched off their original wagon train and headed on to California alone, and during their journey had been ambushed by natives. Most of the family died, and two of the sisters, fourteen-year-old Olive and seven-year-old Mary Ann, had been taken captive and forced to be slaves. After a year, they were traded to the Mohave, and sadly, Mary Ann passed away from starvation during a famine. Olive lived in the tribe for four years. Unknown to her, her oldest brother, Lorenzo, had not been killed in the attack. He had spent all those years searching for her and Mary Ann. Eventually word reached him that, after an exhaustive search, Olive had been spotted living with the Mohaves. Olive and Lorenzo had helped a clergyman write *The Captivity of the Oatman Girls* a year after Olive had left the tribe. It was then the Ross family and most of the country learned of their story. Although Rebecca hated to think of it, they were doing something *very* similar to the Oatman family *very* soon. The Ross and Willoughby families would be leaving the main wagon train and heading deeper into Colorado while the rest headed on toward Oregon. Rebecca looked up and saw the fear on Susan's face. Clearing her throat, Rebecca said encouragingly, "Don't worry, Su, we aren't in Yavapai territory."

"Will we be?"

Rebecca chewed on her lip. "I really don't know. But anyway"—she tried to lighten her voice— "that was thirteen years ago. We're in good old 1863 now. Things have changed since 1850 when the whole incident happened."

Susan raised her eyebrows in disbelief as she nudged Rebecca. "I guess so—things have changed. Now we're just in something along the lines of a major civil war."

Rebecca shook her head with a smirk, then said, "But really, Susan, don't worry about something that's liable not to happen. The main thing we can do to guard against something like that is to be prepared and strong. One of the main reasons the Yavapai attacked the Oatmans is because they saw an opportunity. We won't give them that chance."

"I wouldn't." Reuben added his opinion, a set frown on his face.

"Oh, no, you'd do everything in your power to keep us safe, and"—Rebecca began to laugh— "if you ran out, you'd borrow some of Abe's power."

"Exactly." Reuben pushed back his hat as he asked, "Su, do you still want to turn back?"

She shook her head. "Yes, it still scares me. But I can be brave like the rest of you. I don't want to give up on Pa's dream. And it will be wonderful to live in the same town as Uncle Robert and Aunt Caralee again."

"That's the Susan I know!" Reuben tugged on her hair as he used to when they were little.

Susan smiled and went back to washing her work dress in the singing brook. Reuben said farewell and strolled over to some of his friends. Rebecca grew silent, the subject still bothering her. Yes, Reuben would give his life for every one of his siblings, but against a certain number, it really wouldn't matter. Then, looking into the sky, Rebecca realized they didn't just have a brave brother looking out for them. They had someone much bigger and stronger and able to do more and prevent more than any earthly father or brother ever could. She shut her eyes and whispered, "Thank You, heavenly Father, for being with us."

And then she splashed Susan with a handful of water, expected the payback shot that ran cold water down her spine, and returned to work.

# CHAPTER 5

# Making Plans

As the wagon jostled and jolted around, Emily
sighed. Like everyone, she was tired of riding in a
wagon. It had been over a month since they had
left Independence, and it felt like all the days were
running together. They were now in Colorado
Territory, which was where they were going to settle.
Emily was especially sad because today was the day
they would part with the Sellers, who would not be
traveling to the same town as the Rosses and their
cousins. It had come all too quickly, and she was
dreading the good-byes. Reuben pulled the wagon to
a halt and turned to look back at his siblings.

"This is where we part," he said, eyes darting downward. "Mr. Sellers just motioned they have to break off now."

Two large tears rolled down Anna's cheeks, and her lip wobbled. Like they were attending a funeral, the children slowly climbed out of the wagon and stood with Samuel, Lydia, and Lilly, across from the Sellers.

"Well, we sure have been through a lot together, haven't we now?" Mr. Sellers said, trying to keep his voice light, but it cracked, and Josie let out a sob.

Before anyone could say anything more, Susan rushed forward and embraced Hattie, the oldest Sellers daughter, crying as though her heart would break. Reuben followed her, and solemnly shook hands with seventeen-year-old James. Although they tried to hide it, both of the boys' eyes were glassy. Sarah, Emily, Anna, and Lilly gathered around Ida, who tried to hug them all at once. Joshua squared his shoulders and walked over to Michael and Micah and held out his hand like a grown man. The twins' lips were trembling, and Joshua broke down, and the three embraced. Rebecca and Lydia both embraced Mrs. Sellers tightly, who had been such a mother figure to them when they needed it most.

Abraham patted Christopher on the back and then turned to Josie, opening his mouth, but no words came from it. Josie, her large brown eyes for once not dancing, stepped forward and engulfed him in an embrace.

"I'm going to miss you so much," she whispered in his ear, hiccupping as she cried. "You're like another brother."

Abraham blushed and hugged back. "I'm going to miss you too, Josie. Had I not literally run into and sent you sprawling that day in the general store in Independence, our families would have never known each other."

Josie laughed at the memory and wiped her eyes, giggling as she stepped back. "We've had such fun together, haven't we? I won't forget any of this, I promise."

"I'm going to have a pretty difficult time forgetting this myself," Abraham replied with a smile.

"You've been so good to us," Rebecca said to Mrs. Sellers, hugging her tightly. "We could never repay you."

Mrs. Sellers stroked Rebecca's hair like she was a little girl, and said softly, "I was just doing what I know your ma would have done."

Rebecca smiled. "How would you know what she's like?"

"Because everyone says you are just like her."

Rebecca sobbed, and Mrs. Sellers held her close.

"Don't get into too much trouble, sons," Mr. Sellers said to Samuel and Reuben as they stood by him and James.

Reuben shared a glance with James. "Oh, we can't possibly get in as much trouble as the first day we were on cattle duty on the trail," Reuben answered, smirking, and James rubbed the back of his neck with a laugh.

Mr. Sellers raised an eyebrow as he looked at his son and his friend. "And what would that be?"

Reuben looked at James and asked, "Do you want to tell him, or should I?"

"You, by all means," James replied. "I have to be able to sit down on a wagon seat for the rest of the day."

Reuben smiled and quickly explained, "Well, we were on cattle duty one of the days Abe was driving our wagon, and we got a bit bored, and let's just say we had a momentary lapse in judgment. James and I got this idea that it would be great fun to see if we could ride one of the steers like we saw a passing cowboy do once. We argued over who should be the first to try, but in the end, we found two steers grazing side by side and leapt onto them on the count of three. James missed his steer entirely, and I landed on mine but was quickly bucked off. We had the cattle so flustered they nearly stampeded!"

Mrs. Sellers, overhearing this story, crossed her arms and said, "Is that why James came back from watching the cattle one day with cow dung all down the front of his shirt?"

"It's a lot worse than that, Ma," James replied, crunched over with laughter. "I landed face-first in a fresh patty. I cleaned off most of it in the creek before coming to you!"

Mrs. Sellers swatted playfully at James's rear, and he jumped forward to avoid the blow. All three families were laughing, but as the hysteria tapered off, everyone knew it was time to part. The children exchanged hugs one last time, and Mrs.

Sellers handed a packet of seeds to Rebecca as they embraced.

"They're from my flower garden back home in Arkansas. I kept some for myself, but I want you to have these to plant in front of your new home," she explained softly. "That way you'll always have a piece of our family."

"Thank you so much," Rebecca said, holding the pouch to her chest. "I'll take amazing care of them."

Reuben and Mr. Sellers shook hands one last time, and then the Sellers family climbed into their two wagons, and Mr. Sellers and James flicked the reins. Hattie, Josie, Christopher, Michael, Micah, and Ida waved until the wagons were just a dot on the horizon. It was then, when Rebecca looked over at Reuben, that his face turned into a curious sort of frown, and he opened his right hand. Rebecca watched his face switch from a frown to open shock, and then she saw why. In his hand, pressed there by

Mr. Sellers, was a ten-dollar bill. Rebecca brought her hand to her mouth, and Reuben's eyes filled with tears of gratitude as they gazed out at the horizon, where two wagons were getting farther and farther away.

There was silence as the Rosses' wagon rolled on toward Uncle Robert and Aunt Caralee's house, each turn of the wheels carrying them a greater distance away from the Sellers.

"We need to go back," Anna said, her tone weepy as she stood on the straw tick mattress and tapped Rebecca on the shoulder.

Rebecca swiveled around to look at her little sister. "Why?" she asked in concern.

"We forgot something really important."

"What?" Reuben questioned.

Anna burst into tears and shouted, rubbing her fists in her eyes, "The Sellers! I don't want to go on without them!" She plopped down firmly on the bed and wailed.

"Anna," Rebecca started gently, but stopped as she could feel a lump in her throat. She hid her face in her hands.

"I miss Ida," Emily said very softly, a falter in her voice. Sarah voiced her agreement.

Abraham sighed. "Yeah, and I miss Josie and Christopher."

"And Michael and Micah," Joshua added.

"I can't believe I may never get to talk to Hattie again," Susan whispered sadly. Joshua was the only one who heard her, because they were riding next to each other on Star and Malachi.

"We will all miss them, I know," Rebecca said, her voice breaking. "But keep your chins up. We may see them yet again. Stranger things have happened. Look at how we met them! Abraham literally ran into Josie, and that got the whole friendship started. I wouldn't be surprised if the next time we see them it will be Joshua who drives into their wagon!"

This prompted some moody giggles that dissipated as each thought how low the chance of their meeting again truly was. Reuben was silent as he tugged the reins to the left to avoid a large drop in the trail. It was unusual for everyone to be so quiet and sullen at the same time. Anna wouldn't stop crying, and soon Emily's quiet sniffles joined her. At least the scenery was starting to get a little more interesting; animals like pronghorn were more common as well as buffalo, hare, and magpies. Out on the horses, Joshua and Susan watched the creatures with fascination, though they soon became disinterested after hours more of traveling.

"How much farther do we have to go before we

reach the town your parents are in, Sam?" Reuben finally shouted to his cousin, who was riding in the wagon next to theirs.

"I think that town we see on the horizon is it," Samuel called back. "Since we got an early start today, we should reach it before nightfall."

"I sure am grateful that the days stay lighter for a long while now that we're in June," Rebecca said, letting her bonnet hang from her neck. Her brown hair glistened in the afternoon sun.

"Well, it certainly makes it a whole lot hotter, that's for sure." Abraham groaned, fanning his face with his straw hat. He didn't mean to complain, but everyone was sick of riding in a wagon. They had been traveling for almost three months, and it seemed like trial after trial kept happening to them. He just wanted a break.

"Hotter, yes," Sarah agreed, "but it also makes the katydids sing! And they sing so beautifully."

"You always look on the bright side of everything," Abraham said with a tired frown as he wiped the sweat off his forehead.

Sarah shrugged happily. "I guess I do. I just like it. And I can't wait to meet Uncle Robert and Aunt Caralee. You've all told me so much about them that I feel like I know them!"

Abraham pulled one of Sarah's blond braids. "They will love you."

"I can't believe it's been so many years since we've seen them," Rebecca said from up on the wagon seat. She looked back and saw that Emily was working on her sampler, which was a piece of scrap cloth the girls would practice their stitches on. Emily was practicing her stitches by doing the alphabet, and she was halfway through the letter *E*. Sarah was on the letter *X* on her sampler, which was considered very advanced. "Emily, are you keeping your stitches neat and tight?" Rebecca asked.

Emily bit her lip as she stared at the sloppy cross-stitch she'd been working on. "Um, sort of, I guess."

Rebecca chuckled and said, "Sarah, check Emily's stitches, please."

Sarah leaned over and looked at the lopsided stitches. She knew her younger sister hated redoing stitches. She carefully reported, "Well … they're stitches, that's for *sure.*"

Rebecca shifted her posture to the right without turning her head. "I'll take that as they're messy."

"Yeah, they really are," Emily admitted, preparing to take out the stitches and redo them.

Rebecca, though, stopped her. "Wait, Emily. I know how hard it is to sew in a moving wagon, so don't worry about taking those stitches out. Just work harder on your next ones."

Emily smiled in relief. "Thank you, Becca! I promise I will!"

Anna was sitting on the straw tick mattress,

looking out the back of the wagon. Her little golden braids bounced as the wagon bumped over a rock in the path. "What do Uncle Robert and Aunt Caralee look like, Becca?" she asked.

Rebecca grew silent as she tried to remember. "Honestly, Anna, I don't remember too much. I was . . . nine when they moved away, so I should remember, but I never really paid much attention. They have a little girl named Elizabeth, too . . . well, I guess she's probably not little anymore. She was just a little thing when they moved away from Kentucky, maybe Anna's age or a little younger. That would make her about thirteen now. She was adorable and was always getting into mischief. Which," Rebecca added, looking back at her youngest sister, who was sneakily tying Abraham's shoelaces to a crate as he told a tale to Emily, "reminds me an awful lot of someone I know."

Anna realized Rebecca was on to her, and

she quickly freed Abraham's laces and grinned sheepishly. Rebecca raised her eyebrow, then shook her head with a sigh as she made a signal for Anna to sit down and keep her hands to herself.

"Maybe Elizabeth and I will become friends," Sarah said thoughtfully. "We are cousins, after all." She looked at Anna, who was now sitting dejectedly on the bed with her chin resting in the palm of her hand. "Anna, please may I try to braid your hair again? It's almost long enough now, I think."

"That's what you said last time," Anna muttered, but then consented.

Sarah tried for a moment to twist her little sister's curly blond hair into two small braids, but it was no use. It was too short and too curly. "You must have gotten the curls from our Aunt Edith," Sarah said after some thought. "Remember Pa's sister, Anna? She came and visited us in Missouri when you were tiny."

Anna's face scrunched up in thought. "I don't remember her. How old was I?"

"Well, almost three, so I guess a little too young to remember. She and Uncle Henry and our four cousins came to the farm and stayed there for about a month before they moved out to Oregon."

"She had the curliest hair I've ever seen," Abraham said, floating his hands around his head to demonstrate the volume.

"I don't know about that, Abe," Emily challenged. "Molly Wood had pretty curly hair."

Abraham tickled Emily as he said, "She sure did!"

From her spot on the wagon seat, Rebecca sighed softly.

Sarah, who was sitting directly behind her oldest sister, leaned on the back of the wagon seat with her elbows and said, "You miss Molly, don't you?"

"Yes, I miss all of the Wood family. I wonder how

Jonas is doing in the army, and if Michael Jones has asked Molly to marry him yet. We used to talk about it all the time. We made so many plans together. She wanted to be a schoolteacher, and I wanted to teach others to play the violin." Rebecca cupped her chin in her hands and sighed again. She knew she'd make new friends, but she didn't think any could be as good as Molly. They had been inseparable since they were young.

"Why don't you write to her once we get to our new home? I'm sure she'll write back quickly," Sarah suggested kindly.

Rebecca nodded and looked out at the landscape. "Yes," she answered quietly. "I will write to her as soon as we get settled down, though I do wonder if the town closest to us will have a post office, or some way to send mail. Some of the new towns out here don't, you know. Oh, I'll just die if I can't write to her anymore and will never hear anything of her wedding, or of Jonas's well-being. I don't even want to think about it." Rebecca's voice quivered, and Sarah looked down.

Silence fell over the wagon. Everyone was doing what they usually did, which mainly consisted of staring out the back of the wagon at the prairie, and soon Anna was pestering Sarah to tell her a story about their pa. Rebecca wasn't paying much attention to the goings-on. She looked to be in her own world. She seemed to get like that every time someone mentioned the Wood family. She started thinking about random things, as if she wanted to take her mind off them.

Susan noticed Rebecca's mood when she rode up to the wagon seat on Star. "Thinking about something, Becca?"

"What?" Rebecca jerked out of her daydream. "Oh, uh, sorry, Susan. I was just trying to imagine what kind of house we'll live in on our property. It will be log, and for a while we'll have just two rooms that serve as the kitchen and bedroom. Then, maybe in a few years or so we'll add onto it. We might have a parlor, and possibly two bedrooms instead of one. You know, one for us girls, and another for the boys. And maybe a loft . . ." Rebecca trailed off and shrugged.

"That sounds nice," Susan said, nodding.

Just then, Abraham stuck his head out of the wagon and shouted, "Time's up, Susan! It's my turn to ride Star!"

"All right."

# CHAPTER 6

# Reunion

After the siblings had made the exchange on the horses, things went back to normal. Emily continued to work on her sampler, and Joshua, who had given up his spot on Malachi so Sarah could take a turn, told Anna a riveting tale of a time he got lost at night in the cornfield.

Before they knew it, they had almost reached the town. Everyone was looking forward to seeing real, solid, unmoving structures. What met their eyes was a small cluster of buildings, which, from the looks of it, were only one story high.

"*That* is a town?" Anna inquired in disbelief,

thinking back to Augusta, with its many buildings. This was pitiful in her mind.

Reuben knew how it could feel coming from a large, bustling town, filled with more people than a little girl could meet, to a place that looked barely more than a few stores clumped together on one street. "Yes, Anna. It is a town. Even though it's small, we're lucky there is one. Some places where people are settling don't have a town. They have to rely strictly on the land and have no neighbors."

Anna's mouth fell open. "No town or neighbors at all?"

"Not at all."

"Whoa." Anna's blue eyes grew to the size of saucers. "How is that possible?"

Reuben shrugged and gestured ahead to stress the point. "It just is."

"That don't make no sense," Anna argued, her face puckered up in deep thought.

"That *doesn't* make *any* sense, Anna," Susan corrected gently.

"That's what I said. It don't make no sense. Becca, can I walk alongside the wagon, please?" Anna asked, looking very eager to do so.

Rebecca sighed. "Anna, didn't we just go over this twenty minutes ago? I thought I said to wait. The last time you walked beside the wagon you ended up soiling your dress in that mud puddle, remember? It took me an hour to get the stains out. Let's just try to get to town looking halfway decent."

"I remember, and I know you said to wait, but I just thought it couldn't hurt to ask again," she replied innocently. "Is that naughty?"

Rebecca thought for a second, then replied, "No, it's not naughty."

The wagons rolled on for about a mile more before they reached the town limits. Everyone in the wagon pushed their way up to the wagon seat to

see. It really was a small town, with roughly made
streets called Main Street and South Street. That
was all. Not many people were out, but those who
were turned to look as the wagons passed by. Samuel
shouted to Reuben and said they should ask at the
hotel for directions to his pa's farm. Reuben shouted
back at Samuel to lead the way. The two wagons
pulled to a stop in front of Massengill's Hotel. It was
the only building in all the town that wasn't made
of rough, freshly cut wood. Instead, it was made of
smooth, polished wood and was even painted white.
Sitting on the porch of the hotel was a man of about
fifty dressed in a typical farming outfit: plain brown
pants, suspenders, a grayish-white long-sleeve shirt,
and a straw hat. Susan thought he looked vaguely
familiar, but she couldn't quite place him.

"Pa! Pa!" Samuel frantically shouted with
childlike excitement, jumping down from his wagon
and racing up the steps of the porch and into his

father's arms. His father attempted to lift him up in a bear hug like he would have ten years earlier, but it just resulted in both laughing and tripping over each other.

"Hello, Uncle Robert!" Reuben yclled. He, too, jumped from his spot on the wagon seat and ran to his uncle. The rest of the siblings were quick to follow.

Uncle Robert looked shocked when he saw the Ross children. He let go of Samuel and stared at them, as if he wasn't sure what he was seeing. "Is that you, Reuben?" he asked in a confused voice. "It can't be."

"It's me," Reuben replied, grinning widely as Uncle Robert clasped his hand in a hearty handshake. "It's so good to see you again."

"It's a great surprise to see you all!" Uncle Robert said, looking around at his nieces and nephews with a slight amount of confusion on his face as he searched for the familiar faces of his sister and brother-in-law.

Abraham could tell he was scanning for their parents. The children stood there awkwardly, not really sure what to say. Sarah's eyes were starting to leak, and Emily's chest was silently heaving up and down, as if she was trying not to cry. It was an overwhelming feeling to see a father figure and then be reminded that you had no father, or mother, for that matter.

Finally, Rebecca bit her lip as she said, "Uncle Robert, we sent you a letter telling you what happened . . . didn't you receive it?"

"No, we haven't received anything from your family since Christmas, when your ma sent us an update on how you all were doing," he replied quickly.

Rebecca took a deep breath, dreading that she would have to break the news face-to-face. "Uncle

Robert . . . Pa and Ma passed away from smallpox in February. Th-they went very quickly. They . . . didn't struggle much."

"No, it can't be." Uncle Robert sat down on the steps with a heavy plunk. His mouth was in a thin line, and his eyes were filled with tears. He hid his head in his hands for a moment as he gave a few, quiet sobs.

"We're so sorry you had to find out this way," Susan said quietly, putting a hand on her uncle's shoulder.

"No, no. I'm sorry. I'm so very sorry. How I wish your aunt and I would have known. We would have dropped everything and come to care for you children." Uncle Robert sighed, then wiped his eyes and stood. He opened his arms and took in Susan and Emily, who were nearest him; then the rest gathered around into a large embrace. There was an immediate bond.

They were finally back with family.

"It's okay, Uncle Robert," Anna said, tugging on his shirt as they stepped back. "Rebecca and Reuben have taken good care of us."

Uncle Robert smiled through teary eyes at the sweet young niece he'd never met before. "I'm glad to hear that. But will one of you *please* tell me why you are out here on your own?"

Reuben explained how they were following their pa's dream to move west. Then, along the way, they had run into Samuel and Lydia and found out that they were heading to Colorado Territory to stake a claim.

"So we decided to come with them." Reuben finished up with a smile on his face. It was still a bit of a somber smile, because it never got any easier having to explain to someone what had happened to their parents.

"I see. Well, I'm so glad you did. Your Aunt

Caralee will be so excited—and surprised—to see you. All of you," Uncle Robert said, smiling at the four youngest siblings, "including these fine-looking nieces and nephew that I've yet to meet."

Rebecca got the hint. "Uncle Robert, this is Joshua and Sarah; they're both nine. If you'll remember, they were only a year old when you left Kentucky for Minnesota."

"Sakes alive, those little ones have turned out mighty sharp!" Uncle Robert exclaimed, shaking Joshua's hand and embracing Sarah. "I didn't recognize you!"

Rebecca smiled as Joshua and Sarah giggled. Then she continued with the introductions. "This is Emily; she is six. And this little mischief maker here"—Rebecca tugged her littlest sister's bouncing curl—"is Miss Anna. She's five."

"It is so wonderful to meet all of you. Susan, you are the spitting image of your ma when she was a

young girl," Uncle Robert said as he choked back
tears.

She smiled and flushed a shy pink. "Thank you."

"Hello, Father Willoughby," Lydia greeted. She
and a little girl with curly red hair came out of their
wagon and up the steps to the hotel.

"Ah, hello, Lydia, my girl!" Uncle Robert's face
lit up. "And this beautiful young lady must be Lilly,
the granddaughter I've read so much about in
her mother's lovely detailed letters but haven't yet
had the pleasure of meeting!" He was smiling as
Lilly came over to him and gave him a hug. "Your
grandmother is going to be jealous that I got to hug
our first grandchild before she did!"

"Hiya, Grandfather!" Lilly said with a giggle.

"Well, hello to you too, Lilly!" Uncle Robert
exclaimed.

Lilly grinned and looked up into Uncle Robert's
face. "Grandfather, my nickname is Tiger Lilly! Abe

gave it to me! And I just turned six! Can I give you a nickname?"

"Absolutely, Tiger Lilly . . . but what will it be?"

Lilly frowned and thought for a long minute before saying, "How about D-daddy?"

Uncle Robert swung her through the air. "D-daddy it is! Thank you, Miss Tiger Lilly."

# CHAPTER 7

# Family

"Is Aunt Caralee at your farm?" Abraham asked after a few moments.

"Yes, that she is. She had to stay home to look after Elizabeth while I came here to get some supplies. She believes thirteen is still too young to be left at home. Goodness knows what mischief Lizzy would get herself into if she was left home alone without any supervision. We thought she was old enough, and went to town just a week ago ourselves, and it was an unpleasant surprise when we came home to find her having tea with the goat—in the *parlor!*"

Samuel gave a disbelieving gasp. "Really, Pa? She hasn't grown out of it?" he asked.

Uncle Robert laughed as well. "Nope. She's the same Lizzy you saw all those years ago. Your ma says if she survives to her eighteenth birthday relatively in one piece, she'll be shocked!"

The families laughed.

Looking around, Reuben remarked, "This is a pretty small town."

"Yes, it is," Uncle Robert agreed, nodding. "It's small, but we already have a general store, a hardware store, a schoolhouse, which also serves as the church right now, and, as you can see, a hotel. That was the first thing to go up." He paused, then lightly slapped his forehead with the palm of his hand. "What am I doing? You all must be so tired and hungry! Let's head over to our place. There you can all relax."

"How far away is your 'place,' Uncle Robert?"

Anna asked curiously.

"Oh, not too far at all, my dear. It's only about twenty minutes away."

Anna grabbed Uncle Robert's hand and pulled him toward his horse, which was tied to the hitching post by the hotel's front porch. "Come on then. Let's go!"

Everyone laughed and split up to climb into their wagons and onto the horses. They rode past a couple of small farms before pulling to a stop in front of a small, roughly built claim shanty.

"This is home," Uncle Robert announced, sliding off his horse. He thought for a moment before adding, "Really, I haven't finished it all yet. But it should be done in a couple more weeks."

"It's nice!" Lilly cried as Lydia helped her from the wagon.

Uncle Robert hoisted her into his arms, spinning around. "Glad you think so, Tiger Lilly! Now, let's go inside. Ross children, your aunt is going to be so surprised to see you! I hope she doesn't faint. She is prone to doing that, you know."

The siblings giggled, but tried to be as quiet as possible so their aunt didn't hear them as Uncle Robert opened the front door and Samuel, Lydia, and Lilly stepped into the main room. The siblings waited on the porch.

Uncle Robert called out, "Caralee, Lizzy, I'm back, and I brought you a surprise from town!"

Aunt Caralee came bustling out of a back room, her curly red hair in a braided knot at the top of her head. A young girl came out with her, and their expressions went from shocked to overjoyed. Aunt Caralee ran forward and engulfed her son in an embrace. "Oh, Samuel! I can't believe it! You're here! My goodness, look at you!" She held Samuel at arms' length and examined him closely. "You are so filled out! Lydia has been feeding you well, I see!"

"Ma—" Samuel flushed and rubbed the back of his neck.

Aunt Caralee waved his embarrassment away and turned to her daughter-in-law. "Oh, my dear Lydia, how beautiful you look! And," she gasped as Lilly stepped out from behind her mother and waved shyly, "this must be Lilly! Hello, darling!" She bent down and hugged her granddaughter tightly. "It's so good to finally meet you." Then she looked up at Samuel with a twinkle in her eye. "She got our red hair, Sam. I'm so happy. It's curly just like mine! It's beautiful."

Samuel, Lydia, and Lilly laughed as Aunt Caralee smothered them in kisses and hugs.

The young girl, who had hair in red braids, waited until her mother finished before shouting, "Sam! You're back! I missed you so much!" She ran across the dirt floor to him and jumped into his arms.

He staggered back, gasping. "Hullo, Lizzy! I thought you'd have forgotten all about me after six years!" he teased. "Goodness, you *are* getting heavy."

Lizzy let out a gasp like she was offended, but then she started laughing. Samuel set Lizzy down on the ground and ruffled her hair. She giggled and pushed the loose hair out of her face.

"You're so much taller than the last time I saw you, Lizzy," Samuel said as Lizzy picked up Lilly in an excited hug.

"I'd . . . hope . . . so," she replied, grunting with the effort of holding her new niece, who hugged her around the neck. Lizzy winked at him, then said, "Okay, Lilly, down you go. You're heavy!"

"Like you!" Lilly replied in delight as Lizzy put her down.

Lizzy looked at Samuel in disbelief, then burst into laughter. Lizzy pulled one of Lilly's curls playfully, then gave Lydia an embrace. "It's so good to see you again," she said. "I've missed you ever so much!"

"I've missed you very much too, Lizzy. It's very exciting that we will be living close to you again."

The Ross children stepped into the home while this was happening, and Aunt Caralee was in the middle of a sentence when she turned and saw them. "I still can't—" She stopped, suddenly confused. "Why, who are you?" she exclaimed in bewilderment as the Ross family waved. She took a deeper look at the oldest girl, then whispered, "Is that you, Rebecca?"

"It is," Rebecca answered, and the two ran to embrace.

"I hardly recognized you," Aunt Caralee said, seeming embarrassed that she hadn't realized sooner who they were. "But then I saw your eyes, which are so much your pa's, and I knew it had to be you. You're practically an adult now. When I last saw you,

you were a little girl!"

"Yes, well, a lot can happen in eight years," Rebecca said, motioning for the others to come closer. She gave a brief introduction to each of the siblings, and Aunt Caralee hugged them in turn.

"This is the most wonderful day of my life." She was smiling from ear to ear. She looked around, then asked, "Are your parents still outside? How did they like the trip? I know your ma isn't one for moving a lot. Your pa must have taken a long time to convince her. I cannot wait to see them. It's been so long!"

The siblings looked at each other helplessly. Uncle Robert saw their hesitation, walked over to his wife, and put his arm around her. He then proceeded to tell her about the awful disease that had taken his sister's and brother-in-law's lives. He added that the children had sent them a letter about all this, but it obviously had not arrived.

"Oh, my goodness," Aunt Caralee whispered

softly as she gave each sibling a hug one by one. "You poor children. I'm so sorry! Oh, if only I'd known. I am so glad you moved out here, so we can be close by. We can help you now." She squeezed each one tightly before stepping back to look at them. "Oh, Rebecca, Susan, you two are both beautiful! My, Susan, you look just like your mother did. Dear Rebecca, your voice sounds identical to Martha's. And Reuben, I don't even know what to say to you, young man." Aunt Caralee playfully pointed her finger up at the tall, broad-shouldered boy in front of her. "When I last saw you, you were Joshua's height. Don't you know you aren't supposed to grow so much? If I could put you against your father, I'm not sure I'd be able to tell who is who."

Reuben rubbed the back of his neck shyly and looked at the floor, a smile blooming on his face. The Ross children enjoyed all the comparisons and compliments. It felt, for the first time in months, like they were home.

"Hi, everyone," Lizzy said, once her mother was finished. "I'm so sorry about your ma and pa. They were my favorite aunt and uncle, even though I was very young when I last saw them." Lizzy smiled sadly. "I've heard *loads* of stories about you, Rebecca. And I remember you, even though I was little when we moved. I just seem to remember a time when you and Sam got in so much trouble that you had to scrub the whole house clean! I haven't let him forget any of those stories."

Rebecca laughed. "We've heard loads of stories about you, Lizzy, as well. How old are you now?"

"I am thirteen and a half!" Lizzy turned to Sarah and asked, "Wanna come and see my room? It's up in the loft. It's got a great big window—you can see for miles. Come on!" She grabbed Sarah's wrist and pulled her up the stairs. Emily, Anna, and Lilly followed.

Rebecca and Aunt Caralee smiled.

"I think they are going to get along just fine," Aunt Caralee said softly.

"I think we're all going to get along just fine," Reuben added, shooting a grin at Samuel.

He nodded. "We already are."

# CHAPTER 8

# A Braid in the Shutters

A few minutes later, Rebecca, Lydia, and Susan were helping Aunt Caralee make supper as Uncle Robert showed the boys around the farm. Lizzy, Sarah, Emily, Anna, and Lilly were all playing in Lizzy's room, and the young women downstairs could hear them giggling the entire time.

"What kind of meat is this?" Rebecca inquired as Aunt Caralee handed her a large pot filled with an unfamiliar meat. The greasy mess wasn't repulsive to Rebecca, who had worked with this sort of thing all her life; she was just curious what it was.

Aunt Caralee laughed and wiped her hands on her apron. "It's moose, dear. They're so large we can eat off one for what seems like forever!"

Rebecca set it on the stove and lit a fire as she replied in disbelief, "Really? They are that big?"

Aunt Caralee nodded and tossed some rosemary into the pot. Susan and Lydia were chopping up carrots to add into the meat stew, and Lizzy came downstairs multiple times to ask when dinner would be ready.

After the fifth time, Aunt Caralee placed her hands on her hips and said sternly, "Elizabeth Joannah Willoughby, if you are so eager to eat, why don't you help us cook so it'll go more quickly?"

That was the last the women saw of her in the kitchen.

A few moments of peace and quiet passed. "That worked rather well," Lydia said with a smile as she stirred the stew.

Aunt Caralee chuckled with a shrug. "Susan, do you see that door over there on the opposite wall?" Susan nodded. "That's the pantry. Will you go in there and collect some potatoes and onions? I'd like to put them in the stew. It will make it taste better. Thank you, dear."

"Yes, ma'am." Susan walked over to the door and turned the doorknob. Immediately, her nose was flooded by the smells of herbs, vegetables, and dried fruit. She took her time scanning the shelves for potatoes and onions. There was a bucket of milk sitting on one shelf, and three barrels of flour, sugar, and pickled fish of some sort. There was the crust of a pie in the making resting on one shelf to her right, and a can of Boston baked beans was a delightful surprise for her. Cans were such convenient things! Imagine opening a can and having fresh food without having to do any work. It was like a dream!

"It's almost like our pantry back home," she whispered to herself. She soon found a crate of onions, but somehow the potatoes eluded her. She double- and triple-checked the shelves, but they were nowhere to be seen. "Aunt Caralee," she called, "this is going to sound funny, but I can't find the potatoes anywhere. I'm sure I'm overlooking them somehow, but I just can't seem to find them."

Aunt Caralee came over, her long, pale-green dress swishing. "I thought I still had some," she murmured, searching the shelves. She sighed. "Oh well, I guess we'll have to substitute with turnips." Aunt Caralee picked up a sack and took the onions from Susan. "Thank you anyway, dear."

She took the turnips and onions to Rebecca, who diced them with a large knife on the table. Rebecca passed the pieces to Lydia, who dumped them into a bubbling broth.

"Mama!" Lizzy cried, running down the stairs

from the loft, panic in her voice. "Mama, come quick!"

"What is it, Lizzy?" Aunt Caralee exclaimed, dropping the spoon she was holding. It clattered to the floor as she rushed to her daughter.

Lydia, Rebecca, and Susan shared similar looks of worry.

"It's Emily, Mama! She was trying to see out the open shutters, but then the shutters slammed shut with a big gust of wind. She pulled away quickly, but her braid got caught in between the two shutters. She says it hurts!"

Aunt Caralee and the other girls hurried up to the loft. Emily was wiggling and whimpering as Sarah, Anna, and Lilly stared at the situation cluelessly. Aunt Caralee had to laugh as she said, "Girls, did you think to open the shutters?"

The girls turned bright pink in embarrassment. Sarah looked at Anna with an open mouth, and

Anna grinned while Lilly snickered.

"No," Sarah admitted sheepishly, beginning to giggle.

The rest of the girls laughed along with her.

Her braid still stuck in the shutter, Emily stomped her foot impatiently and said, "Can someone get me out? Please?"

"Lilly, don't laugh at Emily!" Anna cried.

"I'm—I'm not!" Lilly defended, desperately trying not to chortle.

"Are too," Anna demanded.

"Am not!"

"Are."

"Can someone get me out?" Emily asked once again.

Lydia threw open the shutters, freeing Emily's braid. "Here you go, Emily. Better now?"

She nodded and took down her hair. "Yes, thank you. My hair is sore!"

*Emily stomped her foot impatiently and said,*
*"Can someone get me out? Please?"*

"My hair gets sore all the time!" Anna said in agreement.

"How can hair get sore, Anna?" Lilly asked skeptically.

"It just does," Anna replied, crossing her arms.

"I don't know about that," Lilly objected. "My hair never gets sore."

"Yeah, well, you wouldn't know anyhow," Anna shot back.

"Still, hair can't hurt. You're being crazy."

"Don't call me crazy! *You're* crazy!"

Lilly's face turned bright red. "I am not, Anna Ross!"

The other girls laughed. Anna and Lilly were always getting into silly arguments. Never very unkind ones, just ones that didn't make a whole lot of sense.

Just then, the boys came tromping through the front door.

"Ma, is supper ready yet?" Samuel hollered up the loft opening, plopping onto a rocking chair with a relieved sigh.

"It will be soon enough, young man. You just go ahead and set the table since you're so eager, just like your sister," Aunt Caralee yelled back.

Samuel sprung up, turned to his pa, and said in mock dismay, "Pa, I've only been home for an hour and Ma is already putting me to work!"

Uncle Robert chuckled. "Well, don't just stand there! You heard your mother. Get to work!"

Samuel nodded and walked to the door frame, then turned and said, "Abe, you help me."

Abraham threw his hands up in surprise. "What? Are you serious?"

Samuel nodded as he dragged his cousin from the floor. "Of course I am. Come on. If I'm getting pulled into this, then so are you."

"Cousins," Abraham muttered.

# CHAPTER 9

# Remembering Mark

Once supper was ready—and the table set by Abraham and Samuel—Abraham asked Aunt Caralee, "Is there somewhere we can wash up?"

"Yes, Abe. We have a pitcher and basin in the hall by the front door. It's on the small table," she replied, pointing a finger in the general direction.

"Thanks, Aunt Caralee. Ross Family, it's time for supper!" Abraham hollered.

"All right! Supper!" Joshua came thundering down the stairs from Lizzy's room. He skidded to a stop in front of Aunt Caralee and grinned. "Sorry, I know it isn't good manners to be loud in the house. Without Ma and Pa here, we have forgotten a couple smaller rules, I guess. Where can I wash up?"

Aunt Caralee smiled and directed him toward the washstand, where the rest of the two families were waiting their turn to clean up.

"Ladies first," Reuben said, making a low bow and tipping his hat to the girls.

Sarah giggled and curtsied back. "Thank you, Reuben." Sarah poured a little of the water from the pitcher into the basin and cleaned her hands with a bar of slimy homemade soap. Then she rinsed them with the pitcher and dried her hands on the towel that was lying on the table next to the basin. Sarah moved aside to let Rebecca go. The pitcher of water made it through all the girls and Joshua, but when Abraham went to pour some in the bowl for his turn, he found it empty.

"Uncle Robert," he asked. "Do you have a bucket to refill the pitcher with?"

"Yes. Lizzy can fetch it for you. Elizabeth?" Uncle Robert called.

"Yes, Pa?" She hurried over from where she had been helping Aunt Caralee fill glasses of water.

"Will you refill the pitcher with water from the bucket, please?"

Lizzy shook her head. "We're out of water, Pa. I just filled the last glass, and that was all we had. I could go get some more from the well, if you want."

"Thank you, Elizabeth."

Abraham cleared his throat. "I can draw the water for you, Lizzy, if you'll show me the well."

Lizzy's face lit up. "Thanks, Abe. I do have trouble pulling it up from the ground."

Uncle Robert patted Abraham on the back as he and Lizzy made their way out the door. "That's very kind of you, Abraham."

Abraham shrugged humbly. "Well, it's natural when you have five sisters. That was something Pa always made sure we knew: help the girls."

"Well, that's a very good trait to have."

"My brother, Mark, used to do that too," Lizzy said softly.

Abraham looked at her shyly as he responded, "I guess I'll help you out for now."

He and Lizzy walked outside into the warm summer air. It was a perfect day. The sun was shining, the temperature was not too cold and not too hot, and birds were singing. The two cousins tromped on in silence, enjoying the scenery and not sure what to say.

Lizzy broke the silence. "Abe, I have just one question: how do you stay so happy? If my parents died, it'd be like my whole world collapsed. It felt like that when we got the word that Mark was killed last May."

There was another wave of silence as the two stopped walking for the moment. The one figure, not yet a man and barely a child, was struggling with how to answer, and the girl, feeling the sting of the mention of her brother's death from her own mouth, was controlling her tears. A rat snake slithered through the grass in front of them. Everything else paused in time.

Finally, Lizzy asked, "Abraham, are you all right?"

Abraham shrugged, lost in his memories. "I guess so. Ma and Pa always taught us that if something happened to them, the rest of us had to keep going and trusting God. That would make all the difference. It does. And I'm really sorry about your brother. My whole family was so sad when we got the letter from your parents. It must be hard. I'm so close with all my siblings that I can't imagine—I don't *want* to imagine—what life would be like if something happened to one of them."

Lizzy nodded. "It's the hardest thing I think I'll ever go through, but we know he's in heaven, so that helps. Still, it's hard to grasp that it's been over a year since he died."

"Wow. It's been that long?" Abraham murmured partly to himself.

Lizzy sighed. "I get you. It feels like it's been centuries, but also just a day or two. When we first got the news . . . I used to pretend like it wasn't real, like my brother would still come back. My stubborn streak at its best, I guess. I was determined that it never happened. For the first few days I shut myself in my room and wouldn't talk to anybody. I wouldn't eat, could hardly sleep; I just kept thinking of Mark and his laugh. I couldn't believe that not another laugh or even chuckle would come out of his mouth. After the initial shock passed, I used to imagine the day when Mark would walk back into the house and yell, 'Surprise! I'm home! Let's go race the horses, my Busy Lizzy.' But after a few months . . . I gave up hoping and imagining. I had to face the truth. I know it sounds silly, but I just didn't want to accept that my brother, my playmate, my best friend—was gone. That he was never coming back and I'd never get to see his smile, hear his laugh, or get a hug from him again. I am glad that I will see him again one day, but . . . it's . . . it's just really hard since I'm left down here and he's up there." Lizzy pulled out her handkerchief and pressed it against her eyes vigorously, as if to force them to stop producing tears.

"Yeah, I know what you mean. I used to imagine that about Ma and Pa too. When they were alive, it was hard to imagine what life would be like without them. But now that they're gone, it's hard to remember life with them. It's the strangest thing, and I . . . I don't know. I'm sorry, Lizzy."

"It's okay, Abraham," Lizzy said, barely getting the words out. "It's nice to be able to tell someone how I feel. I don't tell Ma and Pa because I hate to see them cry. When Pa cries . . . it scares me. I don't know why, it just feels . . ." She shuddered and stopped.

Abraham didn't say anything; he just reached out and rubbed her back for a second.

Lizzy wiped her eyes again and said, "Thank you, Abraham. You're a good cousin."

He ducked his head. "Well now, I was thinking the same thing about you."

By then, the two had reached the well. It wasn't a very nice well, just a hole in the ground with a wooden lid covering it. Abraham pulled the lid off and lowered a bucket tied to a rope deep into the well until he felt that it was full. He heaved it back up, then untied it from the rope. The two made their way back to the farm house.

Abraham stopped before going in and said as he gazed out at the plains, "It sure is a pretty land."

"And now it's your land as well," Lizzy added softly.

Abraham grinned. "Our land. That sounds like a dream come true."

It was like a spell of beauty came over both, and they stood there, staring out at the beautiful countryside.

"I felt the exact same way when we first arrived here two years ago," Lizzy said, her brown eyes sparkling with diamond tears. "There's so much hope here. But honestly, there is hope all around if we just look. It's just sometimes . . ."

"Buried below," Abraham finished.

Lizzy nodded and looked at the sky.

The wind, playful and warm, blew across the cousins' faces.

Abraham admired the view before repeating

softly, "Our land. It really *is* a dream come true."
He sighed in contentment and shook himself out of
the daydream. "Come on, Lizzy. Let's go inside and
enjoy some supper."

Lizzy raised her eyebrow. "Absolutely, Abraham.
Just one question."

"What?"

"How much moose meat can you eat?"

"Moose meat? You eat those things?"

Lizzy grinned. "We sure do! Hey, after supper,
how about I take you down to the marsh? You can
always find some moose there. They are real pretty
creatures. And huge. They are *really* huge. What do
you think about that plan?"

"Can the others come?" Abraham asked.

Lizzy nodded. "If they want to come, then who
am I to stop them?"

She laughed and raced inside, Abraham on her
heels, splashing water across the floor.

# CHAPTER 10

# Moose in the Marsh

As soon as supper was finished, Lizzy, Abraham, Joshua, Sarah, Emily, Anna, and Lilly headed out to find a moose.

"What does a moose look like, Aunt Elizabeth?" Lilly asked.

Lizzy began to laugh. "Lilly, it's just Lizzy to you. I'm only eight years older than you, after all! Just the sound of Aunt Elizabeth makes me feel old."

"Okay, Just Lizzy," Lilly said with a sly giggle.

All seven children burst out laughing. Then Lizzy motioned for them to be quiet. The group fell silent and instead studied the changing scenery.

There were more trees where they were now walking than there had been on Uncle Robert's property. Birds were singing, and the wind was rustling through the leaves. And if one listened closely, they could hear the faint sound of running water. Water larger than a creek but smaller than a river. It was a very peaceful sound and made all the children sigh in contentment.

"We're almost to the marsh," Lizzy whispered, pushing aside a wayward branch in the path. "Everyone, make sure to stick together. It's easy to get lost, and we wouldn't want to surprise a moose by accident, especially a mother and her calf. Mother moose are very protective of their young. There was a moose attack on another farm last week. A couple of people were hurt but fortunately not too badly. Now, follow me. There's a good spot to watch them right over here. We'll be mostly hidden, but we'll still have a great view of any animal that may come to eat or drink here. I've seen buffalo, pronghorn, deer, bear, swans, and a lot more. It really is a haven for moose, though. Every time I come, there's always at least one. If none show up after I've dragged all of you out here, I'm going to start thinking the moose have it out for me!"

Abraham chuckled.

Lizzy led them to a small bank of the river. Then she motioned for everyone to kneel. The children sat down and watched breathlessly, waiting for a moose to appear. They were nearly completely hidden by the overhanging bushes but had a perfect view of the marsh, like Lizzy had said. Everyone watched eagerly. Ten minutes passed. Fifteen. Joshua busied himself by watching a spider build its web in front of him. Everyone was getting a bit bored.

"Can we go now?" Lilly asked impatiently.

"Hang on," Lizzy replied, mangling a blade of grass in her boredom. "Really, I promise there will be one soon enough. Be patient."

After a few more minutes of silence, out from the underbrush stepped a mother moose and her calf. The mother looked around as the baby frolicked in and out of the water right in front of the cousins. The calf's eyes were big and adorable, making Sarah, Emily, Anna, and Lilly all coo over him.

"Shh! Don't any of you move a muscle," Lizzy instructed in a whisper, as the mother looked directly where they were sitting.

The children froze, only their eyes darting back and forth. The mother soon looked away, and they sighed in relief. They watched as the moose family drank from the river and then ate some river plants before disappearing back into the trees.

"Wow!" Anna said in delight, standing from the ground. "That was amazing!"

"Amazing is right," Joshua agreed, his brown eyes sparkling.

*After a few more minutes of silence, out from the underbrush stepped a mother moose and her calf.*

Lizzy began to answer, then quickly ordered, "Oh dear! Everyone, get down again!"

They dropped flat on the ground and held their breath as a huge bull moose with an enormous rack came walking down the river. He snorted as he spotted the group lying on the ground. Lilly whimpered. Everyone knew that moose could be very dangerous. Abraham and Lizzy looked at each other in worry. The bull could hang out at the marsh for a long time, and that meant they wouldn't be able to leave!

*Please, Mr. Moose, go away*, Sarah silently begged. *We need to get home.*

All of a sudden, Emily gave a sharp, quiet little screech. *"Fire ants!"* she hissed, brushing the red creatures off with her hands.

"Ow!" Joshua yelped as an ant bit him on the leg. He slammed his hand over his mouth as the moose jerked. He spotted the angry bugs overflowing a mound of dirt about four feet to his left. He dug his elbow into Abraham's side and nodded with big eyes toward the anthill.

Abraham looked over, then jumped as an ant chomped its incisors into his arm.

Now all of the children were giving muffled shouts and screeches, and wiggling around, all while trying to stay quiet enough so the moose wouldn't hear them.

"Crawl backward!" Lizzy said softly, getting onto her hands and knees. "Once we're out of sight of the marsh, start running home. Come on."

The cousins crawled away from the hiding spot as quickly as they could. Soon, the marsh was out of sight, and Lizzy popped up and said, "All right. We're all good. Now, let's get home."

About a half mile away from the farm, Lilly complained, "My legs are tired. Abe, can I have a piggyback? Please?"

He nodded and let her climb onto his back. "Up you go, Tiger Lilly."

But then Anna voiced her complaints. "Abe, my legs are tired too! I want a piggyback ride with Lilly!"

Abraham stopped walking and frowned thoughtfully. "Anna, I don't have enough room on my back for the both of you. Lilly, do you want to walk?"

"Nope. I want to ride," she stubbornly replied, scratching a welt on her leg.

Abraham sighed and shrugged his shoulders at Lizzy. Her brown eyes lit up, and she smiled as she got on her knees.

"How about I give you a piggyback instead, Anna?" Lizzy offered, pushing her red braids out of the way so Anna didn't grab them on accident.

Anna's blue eyes lit up. "Yes!" she squealed, hopping onto Lizzy's back.

Joshua faked disappointment. "Oh, man. I was going to offer a ride back to the farm."

Sarah grinned mischievously as she said, "How about I get on you? How's that sound?"

Joshua held up his hands and laughed. "No—no, no, no, and no. There is no way you are riding on my back. You're nearly as tall as me!"

Sarah shrugged. "I was just offering."

Joshua smirked and rolled his eyes. "Yeah, right."

Skipping alongside Abraham, Emily said, "That was so much fun. I love it here. Pa and Ma would have loved it as well. It's so beautiful!"

The six other cousins laughed as Emily spun around, making her faded pink dress billow out.

When the children arrived at the farm and saw everyone else sitting out on the porch waiting for them, the Ross siblings all knew without a doubt that they were finally home.

# CHAPTER 11

# Anna Meets Spottie

Anna woke up the next morning and sleepily rubbed her eyes. Her one arm was asleep, making her hands clumsy. Pushing the quilt off the bed and sliding off the straw tick mattress, she stretched and stood up, tottering only the slightest bit.

"Good morning to you, early riser." Aunt Caralee's warm voice came from behind Anna.

Anna turned around and smiled a tired half smile at her aunt, who was holding a glowing kerosene lamp. "Morning. What time is it?" Anna asked with a yawn.

Aunt Caralee set the lamp down on the table and softly replied, "It's five, dear. Everyone except your Uncle Robert, Samuel, and Reuben are still asleep. Let's be quiet and let them sleep, all right, love?"

Anna nodded groggily and plonked down at the kitchen table. She propped her head up with her hands, then looked around. Last night, Samuel's family, as well as the Rosses, had brought the mattresses and quilts from their wagons and into the house. They'd spread out on the main room's floor, taking up nearly all of it. It had been a noisy night with four boys all in the same room, snoring like there was no tomorrow. Even Lilly had been snoring.

Anna yawned again.

Aunt Caralee turned around from the mirror where she was fixing her hair. "Did you sleep well, Anna?"

She shrugged. "Sort of, I guess. Where is Uncle

Robert, Sam, and Reuben?"

"Well, your uncle is in the barn feeding the animals. He likes to get an early start on that."

Anna's body language immediately perked up. "I love the animals. Think I could go out there to the barn?"

Aunt Caralee smiled and nodded. "Well, I don't see why not. But change out of your nightgown first, please. It's rather chilly out there, and I don't want you catching a cold."

Anna nodded and pulled on her dark blue dress. Then she grabbed her coat from where it sat draped over a chair and began to walk out. She paused and asked, "Where are Samuel and Reuben again?"

Aunt Caralee laughed. "You never stop asking questions, do you, my girl?"

Anna yanked on her shoes and shook her head. "No. I like asking questions." She pulled too hard on one shoe and fell back to the floor.

Aunt Caralee patted her on the head. "I know you do, dear. Well, Sam and Reuben wanted to get an early start looking for a good homestead, and once they find a good one, they'll head to the land office in town to file a claim."

"A land office?" Anna piped, standing up. "What's that?"

Aunt Caralee lit another kerosene lamp and hung it on the wall. Its soft glow filled the room and made Joshua groan and sit up.

"Time to get up already?" he asked in a croaky voice.

Aunt Caralee bit her lip. "Sorry, Joshua. I didn't mean to wake you. I was just telling Anna what a land office is."

Joshua hopped out of bed. "I'm up. What's this about a land office? Are Sam and Reuben staking a claim without me?"

Aunt Caralee nodded. "I'm afraid so, Joshua."

"Aw, shucks! I wish I could have gone." Joshua sighed and crossed his arms. "I thought I asked them to wake me up so I could come."

Anna stomped her foot impatiently, forgotten by the door. "What is a land office, Aunt Caralee? I want to know so then I can go out to the barn!"

Aunt Caralee patted Anna on the head. "Oh, my dear little Anna, patience is becoming. Impatience is not. Well, a land office is the place in town where Reuben and Samuel will go to file a claim. It means they are telling the government they are willing to try to live on the one hundred and sixty acres and improve on it for five years. If they succeed, the government will give them the land for free. Well, other than a ten-dollar filing fee. It's called the Homestead Act."

"That's interesting, but I'm going outside now." Anna threw open the door and ran outside.

Aunt Caralee and Joshua laughed softly and

watched her from the door.

The morning air was cool, and the fog washed over Anna like a rainstorm. It felt like . . . freedom. Anna spun around and laughed and yelled and giggled, because there was no one to tell her to be quiet.

"This is amazing!" she shouted into the wet morning air. She giggled again and spread her arms wide. "I love it here!"

"So do I," a little voice, soft and simple, said from behind Anna.

Anna turned around and blinked in surprise. Standing in the fog was a little native girl. Her long black hair was loosely braided, and feather earrings hung from her ears. Her dress was of deerskin, and it reached her knees.

Anna waved shyly. "Hi."

The girl looked at Anna warmly. "Hello. I am Little Bird."

Anna's face crumpled in thought. "That's a really pretty name, but why a little bird?"

Little Bird shrugged. "My mother is Great Bird. I am named in her honor, so I am Little Bird. What is your name?"

"Anna."

Little Bird nodded to Anna. "A very nice name. What is its meaning?"

Anna shrugged. "I don't think it means anything. It was my grandmother's name."

Little Bird smiled. "Well, it is very pretty. Do you live here?"

Anna shook her head. "No." She paused, then added after some thought, "Well, I sort of do. My older brothers and sisters moved us out here. But this is my uncle's farm. My family is going to stay here for a couple days or weeks before we move into our own house."

A soft call similar to a bird's rode the wind. Little

Bird lifted her head and listened closely. "That is my father's call. I must go back to my tribe. Good-bye, Anna. Maybe we shall meet again."

Anna waved. "Maybe we will. Bye, Little Bird."

The black-haired girl disappeared into the fog. Anna giggled again and did a high kick. She felt so free and safe here on the open plain. She grinned and ran through the dewy grass to the barn. Walking through the door, she called, "Uncle Robert, it's me, Anna. Can I watch you feed the animals?"

Uncle Robert popped out of a stall, waving a towel at her. "Hullo, Anna, my girl! You are quite the early bird!"

Anna frowned. "I'm a girl, not a bird," she said, completely confused by the saying.

Uncle Robert laughed and took her tiny hand in his rough one. "It means you are up earlier than most people. It doesn't mean you're a bird. Did you sleep well last night?"

"I sure did. It was nice to sleep in a house for once. What are you doing, Uncle Robert? What kind of animals do you have here?"

"Well, I'll let you see for yourself. Come with me. I think you'll like these animals especially."

Anna skipped alongside Uncle Robert and chattered on about random topics. She stopped short and squealed when she saw what Uncle Robert was showing her. A large collie dog was lying in one stall in the straw, and beside her were eight adorable puppies.

"They're so cute!" Anna whispered. She watched the wriggling puppies scoot around, whimpering and wrestling. "How old are they?"

"Just over two months," Uncle Robert softly replied, leaning on the stall door. "The mother's name is Coal. She's our collie. We're only going to keep one of the puppies, so the others—"

"Will need a home!" Anna cried in delight.

One of the puppies barked and looked up at Anna. Its eyes were big and brown, and it was black with a white spot over its eye. Anna giggled and reached over the stall door to pet it.

Uncle Robert smiled at his youngest niece. "That's the leader of the litter. He's a little boy. Lizzy's taken to calling him Spottie, because of the spot over his eye."

Anna sighed dreamily. "We used to have a collie. I don't remember her very much. Her name was Pepper. I really like Spottie. Does he need a home?"

Uncle Robert patted her head. "I think he just found one."

Anna gasped and clapped her hands, anticipating his answer. "I can have him?"

"Absolutely . . . as long as Rebecca and Reuben say yes."

# CHAPTER 12

# Old Friend in a New Place

Joshua skipped into the barn, followed by Abraham, who still looked half asleep. Abraham patted Anna's head groggily. "Good morning, little sis. You sure are up early."

"I like being up early," she replied with a giggle. "You look like you want to be back in bed."

"I do," Abraham responded, yawning and stretching. He blinked a few times and shook his head, scratching the ant bite on his arm. It usually took him a long time to fully wake up in the morning.

"We're ready to help you with the chores, Uncle Robert," Joshua said, a soft bounce in his voice. He always woke up more quickly than any of the other siblings, and he had more than enough energy the entire day.

Uncle Robert nodded and motioned toward the wooden feed buckets. Abraham picked one up and strolled over to Star's stall.

Anna grabbed Joshua's hand and sang out, "Follow me! I've got something to show you!" She pulled him along like a little ox.

Finally, Joshua yanked his hand free and said, "Anna, I can follow you without you pulling my wrist so hard. I need it for other things."

"Okay. Come on!"

Joshua ran after Anna to the stall with the puppies. "Aw, puppies! Wow. They are cute!" he exclaimed. He leaned over the stall and patted

Spottie on the head. Spottie whined happily, wagging his tail so hard it looked as if he might tip himself over.

"Uncle Robert said we can have the one with the spot over his eye if Rebecca and Reuben are okay with it," Anna told him with a hug around the waist. "Do you think they will say yes? Oh, Joshua, I really want Spottie!"

Joshua looked down at the little puppy who was staring up at him with his big brown eyes. His heart melted. "I really want Spottie, too, Anna. I sure miss having a dog around. Hey! How about this? Reuben's birthday is only a week away—"

"June twenty-second," Anna clarified.

"So why don't we give him Spottie as a present? He's always talking about how he wants to get another dog once we build our house." Joshua gave Spottie another loving pat on the head.

"That's a great idea, Joshua!" Anna cried, giving

him the biggest hug her five-year-old body could muster.

Joshua laughed shyly. "Well, thanks." He cleared his throat. "Anyhow, I've got to be going. I have to feed Bessie. Abe's got all the horses covered, thankfully. The draft horses are so big, and they get so excited when I come to feed them that I nearly get knocked over! I'll take Bessie any day. Bye, Anna."

Anna smiled as she thought of their sweet red-spotted cow. She was pregnant again. Anna couldn't wait to rub the calf's soft, warm nose and play with it, like she had on their old farm back in Missouri.

*On our farm*—Anna corrected herself in her thoughts—*on Mr. Wilson's farm, right now I could be playing with all those lambs we sold to him. Or I could be at school sitting with Hannah Edwards. She made the best flower bracelets. Or I could be in the front yard jumping Double Dutch with Sarah and Emily. Maybe Susan would join in. I think if we were still at home, she would act younger than she does now. And if Pa and Ma were still alive, I could go sit on Pa's lap and ask him to tell me a story. Or maybe go into the kitchen and convince Ma or Rebecca to let me lick the spoon on the cake batter.* Anna sighed, and her forehead scrunched as she remembered her parents. *Pa looked just like Reuben—with a beard—and Ma looked just like Rebecca—except she had yellow hair like Susan. Or is it the other way around? Do Reuben and Rebecca look like Pa and Ma . . . or did Pa and Ma look like Reuben and Rebecca? My brain hurts.* Although Anna didn't realize it, over the past few months, Reuben and Rebecca had moved into the hole Pa and Ma had left in her heart when they'd died.

Deciding that she was getting bored in the barn, Anna hurried back to the house. Before she went in, she looked up at the sky and whispered, "God, thank you for getting us here safely, and tell Ma and Pa I said that I miss them."

Then, with a smile on her lips and a skip in her step, Anna bounced into the house. Everyone was finally awake and running about.

Lilly ran up to Anna when she saw her enter the room. "Where did you go?" she asked. "I thought you disappeared or something!"

Anna shrugged as she went to the wash basin to clean her hands. "I went to the barn."

Lilly's mouth fell open in disbelief. "Without me? Really? Anna, why didn't you wake me?"

"Because you were snoring like an elephant!" Anna teased.

Lilly grinned slyly and splashed some water at Anna's face. She squealed and splashed back.

At breakfast Anna told everyone about the puppies and Joshua's idea to give one to Reuben for his birthday.

Lizzy's eyes lit up. "That's a great idea! I really want Spottie to go to a good home. What's better than a home with a family?"

"Maybe a house made of a thousand bones," Sarah quipped as she braided her long blond hair into two double braids.

The family giggled. Then Rebecca gave her approval. Sarah and Anna grabbed hands in delight and spun around in a circle, shouting, "We're going to get a dog! We're going to get a dog!"

"Those puppies were about the cutest thing I've seen in a long time," Rebecca said later as the girls sat in the main room, working on clothing repairs. "Spottie is definitely the most adorable of the litter. He has a big personality for such a small little thing. I have missed having a dog in the house, not just for the security it gives of having a lookout but also just having it for a friend. That was a wonderful idea you had, Joshua. Reuben is going to love him."

"Thanks. Though I think it was a whole lot better of an idea than trying to learn how to knit. How do you like this sort of thing?" Joshua sighed as the knitting needles slipped through his hands and clattered to the ground. "I thought knitting would be fun! This *isn't* fun. You girls make it look so easy!"

Emily tapped him on the arm and softly said with flushed cheeks, "I'm still learning, Joshua. It's not easy."

Joshua grinned. "At least someone is making me feel better."

Susan looked up from the sock she was darning. "You don't have to stay, Joshua," she said, reaching into a woven basket and pulling out a red ball of yarn. She unraveled about six inches of it and set to work adding it into the sock.

"Susan's right," Rebecca agreed. "We aren't forcing you. Here's an idea. Why don't you go and

145

check on the puppies one more—"

Her sentence was cut short by Joshua, who cried, "Thanks, Becca, bye!" He threw down his knitting needles and made a beeline for the door. He disappeared in record time and could be seen from the window sprinting to the barn.

Aunt Caralee watched him go with a sad sort of smile.

Sarah noticed and asked, "What's the matter, Aunt Caralee?"

She shook herself out of her daydream. "Oh, Joshua is just so much like Mark, that's all. Mark tried to knit as well when he was Joshua's age."

Lizzy gave a soft sigh and plunged her needle into the dress she was mending. "I miss him so much. I wish he'd never joined the army. If he'd listened to Pa, he'd still be here. I wish he would have at least considered it, but he was so set on going. Now I just hope the rest of our family and friends who are fighting stay safe."

"I know, dear. So do I."

Jonas, the Rosses' old friend from Missouri came into each of the girls' thoughts. He had been like a brother to all of them, and he had left to join the army the same day as the children left for Colorado Territory. Although they didn't mean to, each girl gave a tiny sigh as they thought of him and wondered if he was all right. If he was killed, it would feel like a part of their family was gone.

Just then, the door flew open, and Joshua came running back in, his brown eyes wide and sparkling. "Girls! Girls! You aren't going to believe it! Reuben and Samuel are back, and guess who they have with them?"

A young man with curly brown hair and laughing eyes stepped into the room, throwing a quick bow for a flourish.

"Jonas Wood!" the sisters cried in shock.

# CHAPTER 13

# Fire

"Jonas! Oh my goodness, you have no idea what a joy it is to see you," Rebecca said, giving a quick hug to her childhood friend.

"It's so good to see all of *you* again," Jonas said happily, returning the embrace, then picking Anna up and swinging her through the air. "You've no idea how much I've missed everyone from home. Man, Joshua, you look taller than the last time I saw you," he added to the nine-year-old.

Joshua grinned. He had been having a growth spurt lately. He studied Jonas. He was dressed in the dark blue uniform of a Union soldier and had on a hat of the same color. Although his outfit was different from the one Joshua was used to seeing on him, his smile was still the same, and his curly brown hair was how it always had been. He was still good old Jonas Wood of Augusta. He laughed and smiled as the Ross children talked over each other in their excitement.

"Why in the world are you here?" Rebecca asked, still in shock, but happier than she had been in months.

"My regiment stopped here for a break for the week to recoup and gather supplies. We're headed to Fort Churchill in Nevada Territory." Jonas set Anna down and ruffled her hair. She grinned at him and yanked his pant leg. Jonas jerked down with it, a surprised expression on his face as he looked at Anna, who giggled. Jonas pulled his pant leg free of Anna's grip and squeezed her shoulder. Anna was given a raised eyebrow from Rebecca, but Jonas shook his head. It was fine.

Emily's face fell, and she spoke very quietly. "Oh. So that means you're leaving us again. I wish you could live in the same town as us like you used to."

Jonas pulled Emily's braid. "I know, but at least we get to spend a little more time together before my regiment must get going. I'm here until Monday."

"That's only five more days," Anna pouted, her lower lip sticking out. "I want you here forever."

Jonas chuckled and looked over at Rebecca and Reuben. "I can see that someone hasn't changed one bit! I know, Anna, that you're upset that I'm leaving soon, but five days are better than none."

Trying to change the subject to something brighter, Rebecca asked, "How did you find Jonas, Reuben?"

Reuben and Jonas looked at each other and burst out laughing. Reuben and Samuel had both come in the house behind Jonas, but had been completely forgotten in the chaos that greeted the three.

"Well, Sam and I were riding into town to go to the land office to file a claim—we found a great one, by the way. It's right on the Colorado River, and there's more trees there than there are here, and—"

Rebecca cleared her throat. "You're getting sidetracked, Reuben."

He blinked. "Oops. Sorry. Anyhow, Sam and I were racing, and then suddenly this young soldier starts to cross the street right where we're about to ride through! I shouted, 'Look out! Horses coming through!'"

Jonas took over the story for Reuben, who was laughing too hard to continue. "I thought I recognized the voice, and sure enough, when I caught a glimpse of the younger rider's face, I said to myself, *If that's not Reuben Ross, I'll eat my hat!*"

Anna giggled at the thought of Jonas chewing on his blue Union hat. That would be disgusting!

"Well, I decided to take a chance with my hat," Jonas continued, grinning at Anna, "so I shouted back at Reuben, 'Reuben Ross, you better not hit me!' It was so funny! The . . . the . . ." Jonas struggled to keep going because of the waves of laughter that were hitting him, Reuben, and Samuel. It was contagious and everyone was practically rolling on the floor. Jonas wiped his eyes and tried to continue. "The look on your face, Reuben! I-It was priceless! I thought I was going to have to catch your eyebrows, they arched so high!"

His laugh, and the joy the siblings felt at finding an old friend in a new place, was so overwhelming that they all laughed and laughed and laughed. After a few moments, the outbreak of hysteria melted away, and the friends looked at each other, still wiping the tears from their faces and trying to catch their breath.

"I like you," Lilly said, hugging Jonas around the

leg.

He blinked in surprise, then said back, "Well, thank you, I like you too. But who are you?"

"Lilly Caralee Ann Willoughby. That's my pa." She pointed to Samuel, who nodded.

Jonas squeezed back a laugh as he said, "Well, Lilly Caralee Ann Willoughby, do you go by all those names?"

"Nope. I'm Lilly, or Tiger Lilly. That's my nickname from Abe. Do you have a lot of names?"

Jonas leaned on the wall and tilted his head back and forth. His easy-going personality fit in perfectly with every inquisitive child and went with every adult as well. "Yes, I do. My full name is Jonas Patrick Henry Wood, but I go by Jonas."

"Good. I like Jonas better."

A chuckle passed through the children.

Just then, Abraham and Uncle Robert came rushing in, pale and gasping. Abraham stopped for a moment in shock when he saw Jonas, but all he said, breathing in and out quickly, was, "Jonas?"

Something was the matter.

Uncle Robert tumbled over his words. "Boys, there's a prairie fire that's coming. Started in a lightning storm up in the mountains. It's coming our way. We need to load up the buckets and try to build a firebreak before it gets here!"

"Oh no, Pa!" Lizzy exclaimed, smacking her hand over her mouth. She leaned on her mother for support.

"Yes, sir!" Reuben, Samuel, and Joshua cried.

"I'll stay and help too, sir," Jonas added as Uncle Robert threw open the front door.

"Thank you, son. We need all the help we can get!" Uncle Robert said, hurrying out into the barnyard.

After the boys left, the Ross girls and Aunt Caralee, Lizzy, Lydia, and Lilly crowded around the front window and looked out at the hazy horizon and the wild red and orange flames licking up trees and running across the grass. A half hour later, the fire had reached the outer limits of the farm. The firebreak wasn't anywhere close to being finished, though Abraham and Samuel were working as hard as they could to dig it as quickly as possible. Abraham slammed his shovel into the ground, and a searing pain shot through his wrist. He had hit a rock. In fact, the ground around the house was filled with buried boulders. There was no time to nurse his wrist, though. The flames were coming, and coming fast, eating up everything in its path. He pushed through the pain and continued to dig, gritting his teeth to keep from crying out. Reuben, Jonas, Uncle Robert, and Joshua tried to beat back the fire with wet feed sacks, but they could not hold it back for long. It was too powerful.

"No." Lizzy gave a small sob as she caught a

*Reuben, Jonas, Uncle Robert, and Joshua tried to beat back the fire with wet feed sacks.*

glimpse through the smoke. "It burned our wheat field. Ma, what'll we do? We worked so hard to plant it all. It's too late in the season to plant more."

Aunt Caralee hugged Lizzy tight, stroking her hair in motherly comfort. "Somehow we'll manage, Lizzy. I just hope the fire doesn't take the house and barn. That would be the greatest loss—and the greatest danger as well."

Lizzy choked down her tears and met her mother's eyes. "Right." She looked out the window again, her tone begging. "Oh please, fire, don't come closer."

Outside, the boys beat out the small flames, trying to buy Abraham and Samuel some more time with the firebreak.

"I don't know how long we can keep it back! Hurry with that trench, son!" Uncle Robert yelled, which came out as more of a loud cough as he inhaled a gasp of smoke.

"We're going as quickly as we can, Pa! There are rocks everywhere!" Samuel shouted back. "Every time I dig my shovel into the ground, I hit one! Pa, we're fighting a losing battle, we can't finish in time!"

Joshua fell backward as the fire made some nuts from the overhanging tree explode on the ground beside him. He stayed motionless for a second in nine-year-old panic. Jonas ran to him, and cried, "Joshua, get up, or you could get burned! Hurry! Are you all right?"

"I'm fine!" Joshua replied, wiping soot off his face. He stood to his feet and took up his wet feed sack again, blinking fast. He rubbed at his eyes. The smoke was making them hurt, and it was hard to breathe. Jonas ushered him out of the way of the approaching flames and watched him scamper to a safer place in the field.

Suddenly, Jonas gave a sharp cry and dropped to the ground as his left pant leg caught fire. As he had helped Joshua get to safety, he hadn't paid attention to how close the fire was. Reuben rushed over to his friend and beat the fire out with his sack.

Reuben's eyes grew huge as he saw that Jonas's leg was burned. "Are you okay?"

Jonas bit his lip and nodded as he struggled to right himself from the ground. "I-I'm all good."

"Are you sure you're okay? That's a nasty burn," Reuben said.

"No time to worry about those things, Reuben. It's just a little burn. Come on, we must get this fire out." Jonas's voice was as husky as Reuben had ever heard it as he touched his pointer finger to the burn mark. He winced, then straightened his shoulders when he noticed Reuben was watching him.

Reuben swallowed hard as his friend limped off, then resumed in fighting the fire. He was definitely in a significant amount of pain, though he refused to admit it. Multiple times, his hand found its way to his calf, then jerked itself away. Reuben knew the burn was bad, and he hoped Jonas wouldn't push the limit and hurt himself worse.

# CHAPTER 14

# In the Nick of Time

Ten minutes later, the fire wasn't slowing at all, and the firebreak was only halfway finished. Uncle Robert was yelling instructions at the boys.

"Samuel, Abraham! Hurry up with the firebreak! It's getting too dangerous for us out here! If we can't hold it back, we'll have to get the girls and head to the marsh! Joshua, careful! You're becoming surrounded by the fire. Reuben, Jonas, beat the fire out by the barn! It's getting too close!"

Looking around, Uncle Robert felt tears sting his eyes. It was no use. The fire was coming ten times faster than they could beat it out. It was encroaching, and he knew that Samuel had been right. They were fighting a losing battle. There just wasn't enough of them beating it out and digging the trench. With a sigh, Uncle Robert ran to the house and shouted in the door, "Caralee, we can't hold the fire! You girls need to get to the marsh. We'll see if we can't save the animals; then we'll meet you there. Hurry! You have to beat the fire!"

Aunt Caralee gasped and gathered a few things in a shawl. Lizzy ran and grabbed her rag doll from her bed, along with a carving of a rabbit; it was the last thing Mark had made for her. Rebecca and the other girls ran and grabbed a few special things out of their trunks, and so did Lydia and Lilly. Sprinting for her mother's painting, the only picture she had of her, Rebecca caught a glimpse of the raging prairie fire through the window.

"We have to go *now!*" Rebecca exclaimed, picking up Anna so they could run faster.

The girls started out the door and made a beeline for the marsh. They could see the boys tirelessly beating at the fire in vain.

Reuben watched them disappear down a hill in the direction of the marsh, then shouted to Uncle Robert, "The girls are going. We should get out of here as well. I can't keep the fire back!"

"Neither can I!" Jonas shouted in agreement.

Uncle Robert took a wild look around, his heart aching at the thought of all the fire would take. "Right. Let's try to save the animals and then—"

"Need some help, Willoughby?" a man's voice yelled from the smoke.

"Johnson! Yes, we need help or our house and barn are gone!" Uncle Robert cried.

Mr. Johnson and five other boys, somewhere between Abraham's and Samuel's ages, jumped from a wagon armed with buckets and wet sacks.

"Our farm is fine," Mr. Johnson said as he began

beating out the fire next to Uncle Robert. "But as soon as I saw that it was by your place, I rounded up my sons to come and help."

"I couldn't be more thankful!" Uncle Robert shouted, slapping his neighbor on the back.

After the Johnson men showed up, the firebreak was quickly finished, and the fire around the farm extinguished. All that was left was the blackened, ash-covered ground and the smoky sky.

Jonas and Joshua walked to the marsh to let the girls know they could come back to the house because the fire was out for the most part. In the silence, Joshua couldn't help but notice that Jonas was walking with a large limp, favoring his left leg. He also seemed very confused about where he was going. A few times he almost ran into a tree, and he tripped once on a root he should have seen. He was rubbing at his eyes vigorously and shaking his head.

"You all right, Jonas?" he asked, trying in vain to

dust the soot off himself. It covered him from head to toe.

There was a slight amount of worry in Jonas's voice when he responded, "I'm not sure. Something's really off with my eyesight. I can't see straight." He turned to face Joshua, and the younger boy saw Jonas's eyes were almost completely fogged over. "You're extremely blurry. I can hardly make you out. My eyes are burning and itching. They're probably just irritated from all the smoke."

"I hope so. What happened to your leg?"

"I wasn't paying attention, and my pant caught on fire. It's okay, though. Reuben put it out quickly. I'm more concerned about my eyes."

Joshua raised his eyebrows. "It's just the smoke, right?"

Jonas forced an unnatural chuckle that made Joshua wince, knowing it was completely fake, hiding a wave of pain and worry that wanted to come out. "Well, that's what I'm hoping anyway. Say, where do you think Rebecca and the other girls could be? And where is this marsh? You *were* leading the way, weren't you? I can't see enough to get us anywhere."

Joshua's face crumpled into a frown. He'd thought this was the path Lizzy had taken to get them to the marsh, but now . . . he wasn't so sure. None of the landscape looked familiar. *Wasn't it by the big tree that looked like a moose? No, wait, that was the creek back in Missouri,* Joshua realized. *I think I've gotten us lost.*

Jonas picked up on Joshua's silence and asked, "So . . . I'm guessing that means you have no idea where we're going?"

Joshua ducked his head and nodded. "Yeah," he replied. "I think I'm sort of turned around. I thought this was the path we took yesterday to get to the marsh . . . but I guess I was wrong. Let's retrace our steps and try that other path we saw earlier."

"That sounds good to me." Jonas carefully felt for his footing, then turned around and let Joshua lead.

Sitting on the bank of the marsh, Anna said, "Do you think the fire's out? If not, where are the boys?"

All heads turned to Aunt Caralee, who was sitting with her knees drawn up and her head in her hands. She sighed, then looked up. Aunt Caralee's brown eyes were worried and filled with tears of fear for her family. "I don't know, Anna. I hope and pray the fire's out, but there is no way to know. We'll stay here until the boys come and tell us otherwise."

The girls looked around. The marsh still looked the same, other than the smoky haze that filled the air. Birds were still softly singing, but thankfully there were no moose coming to get a drink at the moment.

"Can we do something?" Anna asked impatiently a couple of minutes later. "I'm bored."

Lizzy sighed and threw a pebble into the marsh. "I'm not bored, but the silence gives me too much time to think. What if—"

"The boys will be fine, Elizabeth," Aunt Caralee said, reaching to give her a hug. Lizzy hid her face in her mother's shoulder.

"But what if they aren't, just like Mark wasn't? You said he would be all right, but he wasn't, and now we'll never get him back." She let out a sob.

"Elizabeth." Aunt Caralee reached out to her hurting daughter, the pain on her face easy to see. "I know I was wrong about Mark, but . . . but how could I have known?"

"I know you couldn't have known, Ma. I know you were just trying to be hopeful. None of us wanted him to leave," Lizzy said, wiping her eyes and sniffling. "It's just really hard to be hopeful again when something bad has already happened."

Aunt Caralee looked down at her folded hands, then shook her head. "Elizabeth, I understand that it's hard to be hopeful when your world turns upside down. I have faith that God will never leave us or forsake us. And I know we'll see Mark again one day in heaven."

Lizzy glanced away and nodded, tears pressing at the back of her eyes.

"How about we sing a song or something?" Susan quietly suggested.

The others voiced their agreement. Together the girls sang a soft hymn. The older girls sang quietly, and the younger girls—mainly Anna and Lilly—sang loudly with much gusto. Unknown to them, they sang so loudly that Jonas and Joshua heard them and were able to follow their voices to the marsh.

"Jonas! Joshua!" Rebecca cried in delight as the boys came into view. She ran forward and caught her little brother in a tight hug. "If I would have had more time to think clearly, there would have been no chance I would have let you fight that fire, Joshua. Are you all right?"

"I'm fine, Becca." Joshua grinned.

Rebecca smiled at him and whispered, "I'm proud of you."

"Thanks."

Rebecca looked at Jonas and asked, "Is everyone all right? Were you able to save the farm?"

Jonas smiled and nodded. Then he sat down for a moment because his leg was throbbing and he could see nothing but shadows of the people he knew. No one noticed that he was grimacing as they talked excitedly in their relief. No one except Rebecca. She walked over and sat down beside him, sweeping her dress under her.

"Jonas, are you all right? You look like you're hurt." Her voice was soft and concerned.

He looked over and smiled at Rebecca. Although he couldn't see them, he knew her dark eyes would be worried, and he didn't want that worry to deepen. "I'm fine, Becca. I got a small burn on my leg, but it's nothing serious. I should be right as rain in a couple of days or so. It's not too bad, but it's causing some decent pain right now. I'm sure that's just because it's fresh."

Rebecca's eyebrows creased inward as she went to touch the wound. "Oh, Jonas. I'm so sorry. Is there anything I can do to help it feel better? Here, let me take a look at it."

He waved her concern away. "I'm fine. Really."

Rebecca shook her head, unconvinced, then asked, "Was the farm badly damaged?"

"I . . . don't know," he admitted, rubbing his eyes.

"What do you mean by that? You saw it, didn't

you?"

"Not exactly."

Rebecca frowned and stared into her friend's eyes. They were red and irritated and almost clouded over. "What happened to your eyes?" she exclaimed in dismay.

"I think the smoke just made them mad. It's nothing serious," Jonas assured her.

"Nothing serious? Jonas, just how much can you actually see right now?"

Jonas bit his lip and hesitated. He blinked his eyes, trying to get them into focus, but all he could see was a blurry image of Rebecca. "Uh . . . not much?" he said slowly, wincing.

"Jonas, you mean you can't see at all?" Rebecca asked, a slight amount of panic in her voice.

"No, no," Jonas replied quickly. "I just mean it's kind of blurry. It's nothing."

"Did the smoke damage your eyes?"

"I hope not." Jonas shrugged, then resumed his usual tough manner. He stood up and dusted off, then helped Rebecca to her feet, grimacing as he did so.

She put her hands on her hips. "You didn't have to do that, Jonas, you know. You're hurt."

"It doesn't matter if I'm hurt or not. It's a pleasure to do so."

She touched his arm. "Thank you." Then, losing her gentle tone, she smiled impishly at him and said, "You look like you should be a chimney sweep."

Jonas cleared his throat in embarrassment, though he didn't know why. "Uh, thanks, or something like that. Okay, everybody. Let's get back to the farm."

"Em, are you okay?" Joshua asked. "You don't look so good."

Everyone turned to Emily. Her eyes were glassy, and her cheeks were flushed bright pink. She shook her head in a bit of a daze.

"Emily?" Rebecca asked in concern, reaching out to her younger sister. "Emily, what's the matter?"

"I don't feel good. Bec . . ." She trailed off as she passed out.

Susan had somehow anticipated her sister fainting and jumped to her rescue, catching her in her arms as she fell toward the ground. She gasped as her hands touched her skin.

"She's burning up with fever!" Susan exclaimed, looking down at her little sister and then up at Aunt Caralee and Rebecca.

Aunt Caralee's usually rosy complexion was paste white. "We need to get her home. Goodness, how did she feel so unwell and not tell us?"

Rebecca's eyes were filled with tears. "It's just like her," she said in a whisper. "She just goes on about her day and tries not to make a fuss. She never wants to bring any attention to herself." Rebecca gave a small sob as she felt her sister's burning forehead. "Poor Emily."

Susan carefully shifted Emily in her arms. "I can carry her back to the farm."

"But the house is a mile away," Lizzy said, standing and pulling up Lilly and Anna with two hands. "Are you sure you can carry her all that way?"

"We can take turns if Susan gets tired," Rebecca said quickly.

"I can carry her," Jonas offered.

Rebecca looked at him and said quietly, "Thank you, Jonas, but . . . we need someone who can see the path clearly."

Jonas sighed and nodded.

The girls and Jonas followed after Joshua, who led the way. Rebecca couldn't help but notice Jonas's limp and small amount of confusion in his walking, just like Joshua had earlier. But he pushed on like he was perfectly fine. Emily, on the other hand, looked as wilted as a rag doll in Susan's caring arms.

*Lord, please let Emily be okay*, Rebecca whispered in her head.

Struggling to find his footing with each step he took, Jonas prayed the same.

# CHAPTER 15

# Worry and Waiting

When the group finally made it back to the farm, the Johnsons were still there, making sure that there weren't any more sparks lingering in the grass.

Uncle Robert, Samuel, Reuben, and Abraham gasped when they saw Rebecca, who was now carrying Emily. The second youngest Ross sibling was still senseless.

"What happened?" Reuben asked, running up to his sister with deep concern. He touched his sister's head and jerked his hand back to his mouth. "Oh no!"

"Emily's sick with something," Rebecca replied,

looking down at the little girl's red cheeks and strained expression. "She's burning up with a fever."

Uncle Robert gently took Emily into his own arms, murmuring, "My poor girl. Let's get you inside. Caralee, Lydia, Rebecca, you'd better get her comfortable. I'll put her in our bed, Caralee."

Aunt Caralee put her hand to her chin in a nervous manner. "All right, Robert. Come, girls."

Everyone watched them go in, then Mr. Johnson offered to Reuben, "If your uncle needs anyone to fetch a doctor or anything else, tell him the Johnson family is ready to help him. We'll keep your sister in our prayers."

Reuben nodded silently, his broad shoulders slumped. He'd been under so much pressure the past four months that the weight was getting to be too much for him to bear. The hardships never seemed to stop coming. He wanted to be the man his father had been, protecting his family and being strong in every season, but he could only handle so much. He felt hot tears coming up, and he pressed his hand across his eyes and nodded again before turning away.

Susan spoke up, noticing Reuben's abrupt mood change. "Thank you, Mr. Johnson." She lowered her voice and added with a glance back at Reuben, "My brother is under a lot of stress, so I apologize that he is not his usual self right now."

"It is all right, young lady. I understand. And we neighbors like to help each other out when the other gets in trouble. Please do let us know if we can be any help to you. Well, we best get going. Come on, boys."

"Yes, Pa," his five sons replied.

On the way to their wagon, one of the boys stopped next to Susan and said, "I'll be praying for your sister real hard. I lost a twin sister to a sickness ten years ago. I pray it'll be different for—it's Emily, right?"

Susan nodded shyly. "Yes. Thank you, and I'm sorry about your sister." She paused, then introduced herself. "Oh, uh, I'm Susan Ross."

The boy smiled a bit shyly as well. "Nice to meet you, Susan. I'm Judah Johnson."

"It's nice to meet you, too," she replied quietly.

"Did your family just move here?"

"Yes, Robert and Caralee are our uncle and aunt."

"Welcome to Colorado then. How old are—"

"Judah, *wir müssen los!*" Mr. Johnson called.

"Coming, Papa." Judah bobbed his felt hat to Susan. "Sorry, I have to go. It was nice meeting you, Susan. I'll be praying for Emily's full recovery until I hear otherwise."

Susan smiled. "It was nice to meet you as well, Judah. Good-bye."

"Good-bye, Susan." Judah flashed a warm grin,

then ran to his father's wagon and jumped in.

Susan watched the blond-haired boy with a tiny smile on her lips. After the wagon disappeared down a gentle rolling hill, she turned and hurried into the house.

Reuben, Jonas, Abraham, Lizzy, Sarah, Joshua, Lilly, and Anna sat quietly on the front porch so they wouldn't be in the way. Joshua was lying on his back, throwing an acorn at the ceiling, and Reuben, Jonas, Sarah, Lizzy, and Anna sat with their legs hanging off the porch. Lilly was stretched out on the wooden planks.

"How is Emily sick, Reuben?" Anna asked in confusion. "None of us are sick, so I don't get how she's sick. What's she got?"

Reuben shrugged, his brown eyes still worried and not a bit sparkly. "I don't know, Anna," he admitted, his tone husky. He cleared it a couple of times before continuing. "All I know is she has a fever."

Lilly said, lying on her stomach on the front porch, "That doesn't sound good." She flipped over and stared up at the roof.

Reuben looked out at the prairie silently, so Jonas jumped in for him. "Don't worry, Lilly. Emily will be fine."

Lilly threw a rock off the porch, and it hit the side of her parents' wagon. "I hope Emily will get better quickly."

Jonas nodded and ran his hand through his curly brown hair. "I know, Lilly. So do I." Then, standing, he said, "I should really get back to my regiment. We're staying at the hotel, and I'm supposed to be back by now. I'll come back to check on Emily tomorrow, though. And I'll be praying for her."

Jonas straightened to his full height, and Lilly craned her neck looking up at him.

"You're really tall," she said in admiration. "How old are you?"

Jonas chuckled. "Well, Miss Lilly, I just turned seventeen in May."

"When in May?" Lilly asked eagerly, her brown eyes twinkling. "My birthday was May first. I turned six."

Jonas grinned. "I was born eleven days after you, but also eleven years *before* you."

Lilly brushed a wisp of red curls behind her ear. She stood up and measured herself compared to Jonas. "I'm short," she concluded.

Jonas laughed once again. "Well, you'll be tall soon enough, Lilly. Just be patient. I ought to be going now. Like I said, I'll be praying for Emily.

Good-bye, everyone. I'll see you tomorrow."

"Wait," Reuben said, reaching out and snagging his friend's arm right before he missed the porch step. Jonas turned to him, scratching at his eyes. "Let me take you back to town on Malachi, Jonas. I'll take you straight to the hotel."

"You don't have to do that," Jonas said.

"Jonas, you couldn't even see the porch step. You would have gone sprawling. I don't want you getting lost or hurt on your way back to town."

Jonas looked ready to argue, then relented. "Okay. Thanks." The two headed toward the barn.

After a moment, Joshua got up and went to follow him. He tripped getting off the second step and flew face-first into the knee-high grass. Amid snickers from the girls, he popped back up and took off running.

"Jonas, Reuben. Hey guys, wait up!"

The two stopped and waited for Joshua, Reuben's

brown eyes twinkling kindly. He'd seen Joshua's clumsy fall.

"You're getting to be quite the sprinter there, Joshua. I'm not sure I could beat you in a race." Reuben's tone was light and playful like it usually was, but it seemed put on, for once. He bit his lip.

"Thanks, Reuben, but I bet you still could. Jonas, I wish you weren't leaving in five days. I'm going to miss you so much. Can I come to town with you and see your regiment?  Please?" Joshua begged.

"I'm not sure that will work," Jonas replied gently.

"The girls will need you to help them while I'm gone," Reuben added.

"But . . . I want to see the army," Joshua said.

Jonas put his arm around his young friend's shoulder. "You'll see it before I leave, I promise."

"Okay." Joshua paused, then squeaked, "Will Emily be all right?"

"All we can do is pray." Reuben patted his little brother on the head.

"Take good care of all those siblings of yours," Jonas added. He smiled. "And don't worry, I'll be around. Just like when I said good-bye to you back in Augusta. Remember what Reuben and I said the day we came to help find Rebecca and Abe?"

"Yes. 'If we don't see each other again on this side, at least we'll see each other in heaven,' right?" Joshua said, lost in memory. "That was the last thing Pa said to me as well."

"It was?" Jonas asked. He didn't remember ever hearing that story.

"Yes." Joshua looked out at the burned fields. "He said it to Rebecca and me right before your parents took us in," Joshua said softly, making himself look as tall as he could. "You guys should probably go."

"You're right. See you when I get back," Reuben

said, smiling at him.

"Good-bye," Jonas said. "See you tomorrow. Say bye to Rebecca for me."

"Sure thing," Joshua said slowly. He waved as the two boys walked off, then looked over at the house where Rebecca was watching from the doorway. Joshua looked at Jonas and then back at his sister. He grinned.

# CHAPTER 16

# Going for the Doctor

The rest of the day was quiet and filled with worry. The younger children tried to stay outside as much as possible, only coming in the house for meals. Rebecca felt like the saying "when it rains, it pours" was very true that day. Not only was Emily sick, but one of the Ross children's draft horses, Kettie, went into labor that night. That meant Reuben was sleeping in the barn to make sure everything turned out all right for the mother and baby.

The next morning, everyone woke tired and

groggy. Emily was worse when day broke, still burning with fever. Whenever Rebecca, Aunt Caralee, Susan, or Lydia came out of the main bedroom to get some herbs from the pantry, their faces were strained and worried.

Joshua's brown eyes grew to the max when Aunt Caralee hurried out of the bedroom and said, "Rob, Emily needs a doctor. Will you please go to town and fetch Doctor Vendette?"

Uncle Robert nodded and pulled on his coat, asking Abraham to help him saddle his horse. Joshua watched him from the window, his nose pressed against it so when he pulled away, a smudge was left on the glass. He scrubbed at it with his sleeve and frowned.

Ten minutes later, Reuben came into the house, smiling the slightest bit.

"Did Kettie have her baby?" Joshua softly asked, tugging on his brother's shirt.

He looked down at Joshua and nodded. "She had a beautiful foal, a healthy little thing."

"A girl!" Joshua exclaimed in delight. "Oh, I can't wait to see her." He paused, then added, "Uncle Robert is getting a doctor."

Reuben smiled reassuingly. "Well, then, Emily's sure to get better quickly." Reuben's eyes always had a little bit of a sparkle in them when he smiled, but it sent Joshua into a panic when he saw that this time there was no sparkle in Reuben's eyes.

Joshua's lower lip wobbled as he looked up at Reuben and said, "Em will be okay . . . right, Reuben?"

He turned his back to Joshua and leaned on the window frame, staring out thoughtfully. "I hope so, buddy," he said quietly.

"But you don't know, do you?"

Reuben shook his head and looked back at his brother. "No, but . . . I'm praying she's going to be just fine."

"Rebecca and Susan look worried. I wish they didn't have to be. Ma was the one who used to fuss over us when we were sick. Bec and Susan shouldn't have to," Joshua said. He looked so solemn for a nine-year-old.

Reuben put his arm around Joshua and said, "Well, hopefully soon they'll be able to relax. It's going to be wonderful when we have a new home of our own, won't it?"

"Yeah." Joshua gave a small smile. "It'll be nice. This house is really crowded with everyone in it."

Reuben gave Joshua's shoulders a little shake. "It's a good thing you and Abe aren't any taller or this house would feel extremely small. And don't worry, Emily is going to be fine."

Joshua sniffed and wiped his nose with the back of his hand. "Thanks, Reuben. I feel a lot better now."

Reuben ruffled Joshua's brown hair. "I'm glad. Now, how about we find you a good piece of scrap wood so you can practice your carving with your pocket knife? I'll help."

"Okay. That sounds fun." Joshua perked up even more and allowed Reuben to lead him outside to the woodpile.

Around nine in the morning, Sarah followed Rebecca into the pantry as she went to get some herbs.

Rebecca turned around and warned, "Don't get too close to me, Sarah. Not until I'm sure us older girls haven't caught the fever from Emily."

Sarah looked down at her feet. "I know. It's just—I could really use one of your hugs right now.

How is Emily doing?"

Rebecca sighed. "Well . . ." she started to answer. She plucked some feverfew from the hanging herbs before continuing. "I can't really say since I have no idea what she has."

"Is it bad?"

Rebecca pressed her lips together. "I don't know. She's just running a fever. If it breaks in the next day or so, she'll be fine."

"But what if it doesn't break soon?" Sarah questioned timidly.

"Then . . . then it becomes more dangerous. But let's pray it breaks before that point."

"Can we pray right now?"

"Of course."

Sarah and Rebecca both dropped to their knees in the pantry, and Rebecca prayed out loud that God would help their precious little sister. Standing, Rebecca took a deep breath, and Sarah sniffed and looked at her with red eyes.

"No, no, don't make me cry," Rebecca said, starting to laugh as she wiped her eyes. "I was doing so good being strong!"

"I can't help it," Sarah replied, beginning to giggle. They had done this for as long as Sarah could remember. If one of them started crying, it wasn't very long before the other joined in. As their tears slowed, Sarah asked, "Pretend hug?"

Rebecca nodded. "Pretend hug."

And though the sisters embraced the air, it drew them closer.

About an hour later, Uncle Robert walked in and said, "Caralee, Doctor Vendette is with another urgent case right now, but he'll be here soon."

"Another urgent case?" Reuben repeated. "I hope whoever it is will be all right."

Uncle Robert looked at his nephew carefully as he said, "The patient is Jonas."

"What?" the Ross siblings cried together.

"No! What's happened?" Rebecca questioned.

"Well, the blurriness he experienced yesterday after the prairie fire hasn't gone away. His commanding officer called in Doctor Vendette to assess the damage that was done."

"Oh, poor Jonas," Susan whispered.

"Is the damage permanent?" Rebecca asked, tears starting in her eyes.

Uncle Robert stroked his chin. "Well, dear, I can't say. I didn't get the chance to ask the doc. He was right in the middle of the exam. I'm sure he'll tell us when he comes over."

"I hope Jonas is all right," Anna said.

CHAPTER 17

# A Mouse in His Pocket

Silence was all the house was good for now. Lizzy, Sarah, Emily, Anna, and Lilly played checkers, just trying to keep their minds from drifting to the worrisome possibilities. Soon it came time for the afternoon chores.

Uncle Robert stood from his chair and said, "Guess I better go tend to those hollering animals."

Samuel, Reuben, and Abraham volunteered to help, so the four pulled on their boots and tromped outside. Abraham was worried about Emily, but he was also excited to see Kettie's foal. He needed something to take his mind off Emily and Jonas. Uncle Robert opened the barn door and walked in with the boys on his heels.

"Reuben, Abraham, you take care of your animals; Sam, you tend to yours, and I'll see to mine," Uncle Robert instructed as he grabbed a tin bucket off a hook on the barn wall.

"Yes, sir," the three agreed.

Reuben nudged Abraham as they made their way to the back of the barn, where their animals were. "Can you feed Bessie while I feed the horses?" he asked. "Because Kettie's very protective of her foal."

"Okay. I can't wait to see her!" Abraham exclaimed, more loudly than he intended.

The noise by her stall spooked Star, who shied to a corner with a nervous snort.

"Shh!" Reuben warned in a whisper, pressing his finger against his lips. He opened Star's stall door and stepped inside, murmuring soothingly to her. He slowly raised his hand and rubbed Star's long face. "Hey, Starry girl. Easy. No need to be afraid. I'm sorry for the noise. Yeah, that's a good girl." Star nudged at Reuben's pockets, where she knew he sometimes kept sugar cubes. Reuben chuckled and patted her on the side. "Sorry, girl. I don't have any treats for you today. Now, you calm down and I'll bring your dinner in to you soon enough, all right?"

Star neighed. Reuben gave her one more calming pat before slowly backing out of the stall and closing the door behind him.

"I'm sorry for shouting like that, Reuben," Abraham said softly, his cheeks flushed red in embarrassment. "I should have known better."

Reuben grinned at him and started toward Kettie's stall. "You should have." He winked. "It wasn't that big of a deal. Just, uh, try to remember not to shout in the barn again."

"I will." Abraham picked up a metal pail filled with feed off the ground and walked into Bessie's stall.

"Good afternoon to you, Ms. Bessie," he greeted in a bit of a singsong voice. "I'm just going to give you your food, and then I'll be off." Abraham rubbed her side. "I'm excited to meet your baby calf in a couple months. Now hurry up and eat. I've got to help feed the rest of the animals."

Abraham held up the feed bucket to Bessie, and she gladly ate it. Suddenly, a small mouse ran up onto Abraham's shoe and stared up at him with its sparkling black eyes.

"Oh, you'll get eaten," Abraham whispered, remembering back to the day before when he'd caught a glance at the barn's large, sleek calico cat stalking the perimeters of the stables. Before Abraham knew what he was doing, he snatched the little field mouse gently in his hand and put it in his shirt pocket. Bessie finished eating, and Abraham hurried to get out of the barn and release his shirt pocket stowaway. He covered his shirt pocket with his hand so the mouse wouldn't jump out.

Reuben was coming out of Sunny's—one of the draft horses'—stall. His brown boots and lower part of his pants were caked with hay and a little manure. He met Abraham's eye and gave him a nod.

To try to sound like nothing was abnormal, Abraham said, "We finished feeding Bessie."

Reuben looked at him with his teasing grin as he stopped at the entrance to Star's stall. "We?" he questioned. "Abe, do you have a mouse in your pocket or something?"

Abraham turned pale. *How did he guess?* he thought in panic.

He was relieved when Reuben continued, "Or is it ants in your pants?"

Abraham forced a nervous laugh. Then he

started laughing for real. The mouse's long whiskers were poking out of his pocket and tickling his neck. He gently pushed the whiskers back into his pocket. "Uh, great joke, Reuben. Ha. Ha." Abraham forced another nervous laugh. "Now, um, I'm going to run and get something from the mouse—I mean the house!"

He ran out of the barn and nearly bumped into Samuel, who was carrying a pail of milk to the house.

"Whoa! What's the hurry, Abe?" he exclaimed in surprise.

"I, well"—Abraham's voice grew quiet— "I'm releasing a mouse. I caught him in the barn."

Samuel raised his eyebrows. "Let's see the little fella," he said, setting the milk pail on the ground.

Abraham nodded, reached into his pocket, and gently grabbed the little field mouse. He pulled it out and opened his hand to show Samuel.

"Hey, there, little guy," Samuel said with a chuckle. He took the brown mouse out of Abraham's hand and set it on the ground. The little mouse stood on its hind legs for a moment, cocked its head at the two boys as if thanking them for his rescue, then scampered off.

The cousins laughed and walked back to the house. They grew somber as they neared. Inside the cabin, Samuel handed off his milk pail to Sarah, who thanked him and set it by the stove absentmindedly.

"How's Emily doing?" Abraham questioned, stopping to sit by Joshua, who was whittling away at a stick on the porch, though the carving had no particular shape.

Joshua looked up at him, then winced as his pocket knife slipped off the wood and nicked his finger.

"You okay?" Abraham asked his younger brother.

"I'm fine. And to answer your other question,"

Joshua replied, shoving the hand with the cut into his pant pocket, "I don't really know about Emily. Becca and Susan look worried. That makes me nervous."

Abraham put his arm around Joshua and softly said, "It's okay to be nervous, Joshua. I am too. Sickness can be a frightening thing. But Emily will be okay."

"That's what Reuben said," Joshua murmured, "but now he looks worried too."

Abraham sighed. "I know. We are just all hoping the fever breaks soon. The longer it hangs on, the worse it can be for Emily."

"Will she die?"

Abraham shook his head so quickly it made him dizzy. "No. She's going to be all right."

"You know, Abe," Joshua said quietly, "I've been doing a lot of thinking. I don't think we tell people how much we love them quite enough. Like, if

Rebecca had been eaten by that bear back home, I'd never gotten the chance to tell her that I love her pies. Or if Reuben had drowned in the river, I never would have been able to tell him that I love his laugh. Or if Emily doesn't make it, I'll never be able to thank her for being such a good little sister. I don't want to take you all for granted. So . . . I'll start with you, Abe. I sure am glad you didn't get picked up by that tornado back in Missouri. Then I never could have told you that you're crazy."

"Thanks, Joshua . . . I think." Abraham frowned, then repeated, "Wait, *crazy?*"

"I'm kidding. I meant I love your jokes." Joshua grinned.

Abraham tickled him as he said, "Thanks. And I *think* I love yours too."

"Hey!"

# CHAPTER 18

# Surprise at the Well

A few moments later, Aunt Caralee poked her head out of the cabin and asked, "Abraham, will you run out to the well and draw another bucket of water for me?"

"Yes, ma'am."

When Aunt Caralee closed the door, Abraham nudged Joshua and suggested, "Why don't you go fetch the water? There's a nice view of the marsh from the well."

"Okay." Joshua grinned. He went inside and

tugged on his work boots, which sat by the front door; then he walked outside and jumped off the porch.

Abraham was still sitting with his legs swinging over the edge, and he teased, "At least you didn't fall this time."

"Yeah, thanks!" Joshua responded, shaking his head.

The day was warm, and the sky was clear. It was these kinds of days that Joshua loved the most. If it hadn't been for Emily's sickness, Joshua would have declared the day perfect. The beauty of the day helped him to feel much better, though. It was hard to feel worried when things were so wonderful outside. He walked across the field to the well. The well was not as nice as the one back on the Rosses' old farm in Missouri. This well was just a deep hole in the ground covered by a thick wooden lid. A bucket sat beside it on the ground. Joshua pushed the lid off the well, then grabbed the rope that was attached to the lid and tied it to the bucket's handle. He lowered the bucket into the well, and pulled it back up full of cool water. Joshua lifted the bucket onto the ground and untied the thick rope from the bucket's handle, then picked up the bucket and started to walk back to the house.

Sarah was now sitting next to Abraham on the front porch as Joshua walked into the house. He said over his shoulder to his twin, "I'm going to give this water to Aunt Caralee. Then let's meet up by the back of the barn and see if we can see any animals, all right? Walking around makes you feel *so* much better!"

Sarah nodded and replied with a simple "Meet you there."

Joshua ran into the house and handed the bucket off to Rebecca, who thanked him as she shot him an encouraging smile. Joshua nodded to her and let her know where he was going. He hurried out the door and ran behind the barn, where Sarah was waiting.

Joshua had to conceal a laugh because Sarah was wearing the scuffed brown-leather shoes Susan had passed down to her. It was strange to Joshua because Sarah usually had tidy, small shoes that fit her feet. But her own shoes had worn through, and now she was wearing Susan's old shoes.

Sarah noticed he was staring, and she said with a smirk, "Believe me, Joshua, these weren't my choice. Susan said I had to wear them because of the ash from the fire."

A butterfly landed on Sarah's dress sleeve, which was a faded purple. Sarah sighed. "Poor little thing. I guess my dress is one of the most colorful things left out here."

She was exactly right. The destructive prairie fire had left the distant and nearby hills blackened and bare.

"Do I look silly with these giant shoes on?" Sarah asked as the butterfly fluttered away.

"Aw, Sarah, no! You look just fine in them," Joshua replied.

"Honest, Joshua?" Sarah's smile lit up her face.

"Honest," Joshua answered kindly. While he liked to tease and joke, he was too polite to make fun of anyone, especially any of his sisters.

Sarah grinned. "Thanks, Joshua. You're a great little brother!"

The twins shared a laugh at the well-known family joke. Though they were twins, Sarah had been born exactly two minutes before Joshua. So she always teased him by calling him her "little brother."

Joshua looked ahead and nudged Sarah. "Hey, let's go up that hill! There's still some grass on it, so it must have been missed by the fire."

Sarah nodded and exclaimed, "Okay, come on, then!"

The two ran up the hill, which was about thirty yards away from the barn and even farther from the house. From atop the hill, the siblings could see the thick forest that was refreshingly green. Joshua and Sarah settled down in the spongy brownish-green grass and sighed happy sighs. Suddenly, out of the woods stepped a tall, lean figure. Sarah concealed a scream. It was a native man.

# CHAPTER 19

# Healing Herbs

Joshua's and Sarah's mouths fell open as they scrambled to their feet. The native man had turkey feathers in his black hair and wore buckskin pants. On his shoulder was an animal skin pack. He approached the twins slowly.

Joshua gently pushed Sarah behind him and whispered, "Stay behind me no matter what." He squared his shoulders and took a deep breath, trying to make himself appear taller than he really was.

By now, the man was standing not five feet away from the Ross twins.

"H-Hello," Joshua greeted, his voice shaking.

He couldn't help being nervous. Not every Native American was dangerous, but at the moment he didn't know if this man was safe or not. Every story he had ever heard flashed through his brain in a second, but he shook it away. There was no use panicking until the man gave them something to panic about. Even still, he wished Reuben was standing behind him. "Do you . . . do you come in peace?"

The man nodded. "Yes. My name is Windfeather. You met my daughter, Little Bird."

"You speak English," Joshua said in surprise.

"Yes. My tribe is Cheyenne. We trade with settlers. My daughter said new family came to town. I came to meet them for myself."

Sarah and Joshua frowned thoughtfully.

"We've never met your daughter," Joshua said hesitantly, looking at Sarah with a question in his eyes. *Do you know her?* Sarah was quick to shake her head.

"One of you did. The girl's name was Anna," Windfeather replied.

"Oh," Joshua and Sarah said together.

"That makes sense," Joshua added. "Anna is our little sister. She said she met a girl named Little Bird yesterday morning. I'd forgotten."

"Yes," Windfeather said. "Little Bird told me that story. I came to meet the new settlers. I know Robert Willoughby well."

"That's our Uncle Robert. Anyhow, my name's Joshua. This is Sarah."

She stepped out from behind Joshua and waved shyly. "Hi."

Windfeather nodded to her and pulled the animal skin pack off his shoulder and handed it to Joshua. He took it and opened it. Inside the pack were some greenish-brown leaves. Joshua looked up with a puzzled expression.

"What is it?" he asked Windfeather.

"It is the Cheyenne tribe special blend of herbs. They help with sickness," he answered with a nod of his head. "I heard Willoughby went to get a doctor. Someone is sick. I will trade them with you."

Joshua and Sarah both felt a glimmer of hope. Maybe it would help Emily get better! But what could they trade? The twins looked at each other cluelessly.

Reuben walked out of the barn and closed the door behind him. *Oh, I left the water bucket back behind the barn when I took Bessie out to the creek. Better get it before I forget,* he reminded himself. Reuben walked to the back of the barn, but just as he was bending down to grab the bucket, some movement to his left caught his eye. He looked up and saw that Joshua and Sarah were talking with a tall man. Reuben's eyebrows arched. He jogged up the hill and joined his siblings.

Joshua's brown eyes lit up when he saw his brother. "Oh, hi, Reuben! This is Windfeather, and he lives around here," he explained quickly, relaxing a bit more now that the broad-shouldered boy was beside him.

"Nice to meet you," Reuben said, nodding a greeting.

"It is nice to meet you as well," Windfeather replied with a nod. It caused the turkey feathers in his hair to wave back and forth. "Are you Robert's son?" Windfeather continued. "He often speaks of his son. He seems proud of his boy, as I am of mine."

Reuben shook his head and answered, "No, sir. I'm his nephew, Reuben Ross, and we just moved here a few days ago. What is your son's name?"

"His name is Whitecloud, but in your language we call him Paul. He is in his seventeenth year."

"So, Mr. Windfeather," Joshua started, pointing to the animal skin pack in his hand, "what will you want for these herbs?"

Windfeather looked thoughtful for a moment. "What do you have to trade?" he finally asked.

Joshua, Sarah, and Reuben looked at each other. Then they all started digging through their pockets. Sarah found a thimble, some string, and a button in her apron pocket. Joshua pulled out some fishing line and a pocket knife from his, and Reuben's pockets didn't reveal much better.

"I'm sorry we don't have much to trade," Reuben apologized as Windfeather looked over their options.

"Yes, I don't think I can trade these rare herbs for such small things," Windfeather answered.

Reuben looked disappointed; then he stared up

*Windfeather looked thoughtful for a moment.*
*"What do you have to trade?"*

at their new friend with slightly sad eyes. "There is one more thing I could trade you," he said softly. He reached into his back left pocket and pulled out his hunting knife. The twins stifled a gasp. Reuben's hunting knife was one of his most prized possessions, yet he was willing to give it up for a chance to help Emily. Reuben cradled the knife and its leather sheath in his hands as he was flooded with memories of all the things he had done with it, who had given it to him, and all he might need it for in the future. As he looked at it silently, he realized that the knife really didn't mean that much to him—sure, it had memories, but memories were with and because of his family, and he knew he could afford to lose an inanimate object to save his sister's life. He held it out toward Windfeather.

Windfeather's eyes lit up.

Reuben asked, "Will you trade for this?" He bit his lip, knowing the answer.

Windfeather nodded. "Yes, I will trade!"

"Why did you trade your hunting knife, Reuben?" Joshua asked later as the siblings hurried back to the house.

Reuben sighed. "Because, Joshua. Emily means more to me than any knife—or anything at all—ever could."

Sarah looked up at her big brother in admiration, her blue eyes sparkling with tears. "Reuben, you *are* amazing."

He chuckled and ruffled her hair. "Thanks, Sarah. Now come on, let's get these herbs inside."

The three ran into the house and told everyone what had happened. The family was excited, especially when Uncle Robert said, "Praise the Lord! Those herbs are so rare, but they work so well!"

Everyone looked at each other with hope in their eyes.

There was a sudden knock on the door. Joshua sprung to open it. A man in a leather coat holding a black case came into the main room. He smiled and nodded a greeting to Joshua, who grinned shyly. Uncle Robert jumped to his feet and hurried to the man's side.

"Thank you for coming, Doctor Vendette." Uncle Robert took the doctor's coat and hat from him and hung them on a hook on the wall.

The doctor was a tall man with a brown beard, brown eyes, and rosy cheeks. There was a soft sparkle in his eyes. The Ross children immediately liked him, for he said, "Let me see what I can do for the girl."

"Sir, we just traded with a Cheyenne tribe

member named Windfeather for this," Joshua said quietly, stepping up to the doctor and offering him the satchel. "He said these are herbs that help with sickness. Can you use them for Emily?"

The doctor smiled, and he nodded. "I've seen this mixture before! It works extremely well. May I?"

Joshua nodded and handed the satchel to him.

The doctor patted him on the head and said, "Thank you, son. This will definitely help."

Those words were an encouragement to the Ross children. Maybe Emily would be all right.

"She's just gotta get better," Joshua whispered. "She's just *got* to."

# CHAPTER 20

# The Good Doctor

The Ross siblings and Willoughby families sat quietly in the main room as Doctor Vendette stayed in the bedroom looking after Emily with Rebecca, Aunt Caralee, Lydia, and Susan. Hours passed. The sun began to set in the distant mountains.

"Do you think he will make Emily better?" Sarah asked softly, lying on her back on the braided rug in the middle of the main room.

"I'm praying so," Reuben replied. He was sitting on a stool with his back against the wall. Anna was sitting on his lap, her head resting on his shoulder. Her eyes were shut.

Joshua was lying on his stomach across from Sarah, and Abraham was sitting against the wall. They had brought the chairs in from the table, and Samuel, Lizzy, and Uncle Robert sat in them. Lilly was curled up in her father's lap, sleeping soundly.

Reuben smiled across at Samuel. "Poor Lilly and Anna. This is a lot for them to handle. It's good they're getting some sleep."

"I know." Samuel looked down at his dozing daughter with a slight smile. "They're resilient. Not every five- and six-year-old would survive all that our families have been through. It's good to let them rest."

Reuben rubbed Anna's back as she mumbled in her sleep.

"You children are an inspiration to us all," Uncle Robert said, his eyes shining. "I can't believe how well you have gotten on, even with the tragedy of losing your parents. You never cease to amaze me.

You get along so well, even as siblings."

"Family is the best thing ever created," Abraham said from the corner.

"We love being together," Sarah added, looking up from the game of checkers she and Joshua were playing on the floor. Joshua frowned as Sarah jumped his only king, and she smirked. The younger twin chewed on his lip and scanned the board, weighing his next move carefully. If he made the wrong one, the game would be all but lost.

"Who's winning?" Lizzy dropped to the ground in between them and propped her chin up with her hands.

"Shh!" Joshua held up his hand for silence, then, looking up at Sarah with a twinkle of victory in his eye, lifted a checker piece and placed it on a square.

Without a moment's hesitation, Sarah picked up one of her own playing pieces and jumped not only the piece Joshua had moved, but the remainder of his checkers as well. Joshua's mouth fell open, and Sarah giggled. Lizzy snorted and motioned for someone to set up the board again so she could play a round.

The door to the bedroom opened, and everyone scrambled to their feet as Doctor Vendette walked out of the room, carrying his briefcase. Rebecca and Aunt Caralee followed him.

"How's Emily?" Reuben asked anxiously. Anna was still in his arms, rubbing her eyes and blinking in confusion.

The doctor smiled at them and made an announcement that caused all the family to sigh in relief. "Her fever broke. The worst is behind her. Those herbs you traded for worked wonders."

Sarah hugged Lizzy tightly. Anna cheered groggily. Reuben squeezed her tightly, then set her on the ground and shook Doctor Vendette's hand repeatedly.

"Thank you so much," he said, tears building in his eyes.

Doctor Vendette shook Reuben's hand firmly. "It was my pleasure. I always love a case that is successful. I have too many sad endings in my business. Too many lose too much. This was much needed."

Reuben was silent as he nodded. Rebecca spoke up from the back of the room. "Doctor Vendette, I meant to ask; that young soldier you were working on earlier today, Jonas, will he be all right? He's a dear friend of ours."

Sadness came over the doctor's face. "Ah, him, the poor young man. Such a bright, kind boy. It really is unfortunate."

"What's happened to him?" Rebecca asked painstakingly.

"I'm afraid the smoke badly affected his eyes," Doctor Vendette replied. "He's on bed rest in the hotel. I've got a salve over his eyes. It may help, but how much, I'm not sure. Only time will tell."

"Oh, dear Jonas!" Rebecca exclaimed, her hands pressed to her mouth.

"No," Reuben said quietly.

"He can't go blind," Anna said. "He has to be able to see so he can play with me."

"How long will he be on bed rest?" Joshua asked. "His regiment leaves on Monday. That's only four days away."

"I know," Doctor Vendette agreed, "I'm hoping the salve works quickly. But if his sight doesn't drastically recover by the time his regiment is set to leave, I'll have to sign the papers for his discharge. If he can't see, he can't serve."

There was a moment of sad silence, then Rebecca said, "Reuben, let's visit him tomorrow if Emily is stable enough to be left for a little."

"I agree."

After a moment of silence, Aunt Caralee offered, "Won't you stay for supper, Doctor Vendette? I just pulled a hot chicken potpie out of the oven. You're welcome to join us. It's already past supper time, I'm afraid."

"Thank you. I'd like to, but I know Genevieve will be keeping something hot for me back home. Thank you for the offer, and I hope Emily recovers quickly. I'll come back tomorrow to check her progress." Doctor Vendette pulled on his coat and placed his hat on his head, then walked outside to where his horse and buggy were tied to the porch post.

Rebecca and Reuben followed him out, and Reuben shook his hand again. "Thank you, sir, for helping our sister. You're an answer to prayer!"

"I'm glad I could be of service. I'll see you two tomorrow. Get some rest tonight. From what your aunt has told me, you could use it, and that's the doctor's orders!"

Rebecca and Reuben laughed, then waved as the doctor flicked the reins and his horse leapt forward.

"Phew," Reuben said, putting his arm around Rebecca's shoulders as they watched the beautiful sunset in the far-off mountains. "What a way to get settled into a new place, huh?"

Rebecca smiled. "Why does it seem like we never get a break?"

"We've got one now." Reuben plopped onto the porch step and motioned for Rebecca to join him. They sat there, thanking the Lord that their sister would be all right, gazing out at the pink-and-purple sky until the sun disappeared below the horizon.

# CHAPTER 21

# A Visit to Town

The next afternoon, Rebecca, Reuben, Susan, and
Abraham saddled up Star, Malachi, Johnny, and
Sunny, and rode out toward town. They chatted
and admired the scenery as they went, keeping the
horses in a light trot. They passed a farm with six
young men working out in the field near the road.
They raised their heads to watch the four oldest Ross
siblings ride by, and one of the boys walked toward
the road and yelled, "Susan?"

Susan recognized the voice as Judah Johnson. He
waved as Reuben pulled Malachi to a halt.

"You're the boys who helped us fight the fire two

days ago, aren't you?" Reuben asked, as the girls and Abraham slowed to a stop behind him.

"We are." Judah wiped his hands on his pants and offered his right one to Reuben. "I'm Judah Johnson."

"Reuben Ross," Reuben said, smiling as he shook Judah's hand. Reuben swung his leg over the saddle horn and dismounted, landing in the soil. "I didn't have the pleasure of meeting you the other day. We were so busy in the aftermath that I don't think our paths crossed. If your family hadn't shown up to help, we wouldn't have been able to save the farm."

"We were happy to do it," Judah replied.

"We look to be about the same age. How old are you?"

"Eighteen. You?"

"I'll be turning seventeen next week." Reuben motioned for the others to dismount, and he said,

"This is Rebecca. She's your age. This is Abraham; he's nearly fourteen. And I believe you've already met Susan."

"I have." Judah smiled warmly. "It's a pleasure to meet you four. How is Emily? I've been praying for her. In fact, my whole family has been."

The siblings looked at each other in surprise.

"She's doing much better already," Rebecca said. "The fever broke yesterday evening, and today she's already managed to eat and drink a little. We're very thankful."

"That's good to hear. How many are in your family?" Judah asked. "I didn't really count after the fire. It was slightly chaotic."

"Wasn't it?" Reuben shook his head. "There's eight of us in our family. There used to be ten, but . . . our parents passed away from smallpox in February."

"I'm sorry," Judah said softly, pain in his eyes. "I

had no idea. If my family can ever do anything to help you, just say the word."

"We appreciate it," Reuben said, shaking Judah's hand again. "We're on our way to town right now to visit an injured friend. Maybe you saw him after the fire. He was the boy with the curly dark hair."

"Come to think of it, I did see him. He was wearing a Union uniform, right?"

"That's him. His name is Jonas." Reuben looked down.

"He was injured?" Judah asked, a concerned frown building on his face.

Rebecca nodded. "His eyesight was damaged. He's on bed rest at the hotel. We're going to check on him."

"Oh my. Give him my best," Judah said. "I'll be praying for him."

"Thank you." Reuben gave the signal, and the four pulled themselves back onto the saddles. "Nice meeting you, Judah."

"Good-bye." Judah smiled, tipped his hat to the four, and went to rejoin his brothers and father in the field.

"Well, he seems nice," Rebecca commented as they rode away from the farm.

Reuben, Abraham, and Susan agreed.

"He's got an accent of some sort," Abraham said, frowning as he tried to place it.

Susan thought for a moment and said, "His father used a word or two I didn't know when they were leaving after the fire."

Reuben looked at her and frowned, and Susan was quick to clarify, "No, not a bad word. Just one in a different language. Like . . . French or German or something."

They rode for about ten minutes more before coming into the town. It didn't look as deserted as it had when they'd first arrived in the wagon.

Now people were scurrying about and children ran through the streets, chasing each other, or dogs, or cats, or whatever else there was to chase. The four Ross siblings pulled the horses to a stop in front of the hotel, tying them to the hitching post. They walked forward, and Reuben held the screen door open for the ladies before entering alongside Abraham. There was a front sitting room that they walked into first, which was empty for the time being. There was another door on the opposite wall, which Reuben opened. There was a small desk with a young boy sitting behind it, who frowned in a sour way as the four Ross siblings entered.

"What do you need?" he asked impatiently. He looked about Reuben's age.

"Hello," Reuben said, in almost a question. He wasn't exactly sure he liked this boy. "We're here to visit one of your guests—Jonas Wood?"

"Oh, you mean the blind soldier everyone keeps

fussing over?" the boy drawled in disinterest. "He's upstairs, in the first room to your left. He shares it with a few other soldiers. He's in a rotten mood. Not worth visiting, if you ask me."

"We'll decide that for ourselves, thank you," Reuben said, and he ushered the girls and Abraham to the hall with a row of stairs at the end.

"Well, he was anything but friendly!" Rebecca said, aghast, as they started up the stairs. "I'd go as far as to say he was downright rude!"

"Calm down, Bec," Reuben said.

"I don't want to calm down," Rebecca said. "He shouldn't talk about Jonas so carelessly."

"How can some people be so kind and some be so rude?" Susan asked, frustrated, thinking about the stark differences between their recent encounter with Judah Johnson and this hotel boy.

This question remained unanswered as they reached the top stairs and the hallway after. "First door on the left?" Reuben murmured thoughtfully, and Rebecca nodded.

Reuben knocked, and a voice that didn't belong to Jonas said, "Come in."

Reuben pushed open the door, and there stood by it a young man in a Union uniform. He had dark hair and eyes, and a confused smile was on his face.

"We weren't expecting visitors," he said politely, but he motioned for the Ross siblings to come in. "I suppose you are Jonas's friends, the ones he calls his extended family. He was thrilled beyond belief to have been able to see you again. I'm Frank Steel."

"Pleased to meet you. I'm Reuben Ross." The two shook hands.

"You're in the army as well?" Rebecca asked, as Frank beckoned for her and Susan to sit down on the two chairs in the corner of the room.

"I am. Jonas has become a close friend of mine these past few months. I hate to see this happening to him; I do. He's behind that door there"—Frank nodded toward a small door across from them—"which is the second part of this room. Laurence Hughes and Scottie Paler share it with us. They're in with Jonas right now. So's the doctor." Frank spoke sadly, his head down, not meeting the begging eyes of the children.

"How is he?" Susan asked quietly.

Frank hesitated and looked at Reuben. "He's . . . he's taking it like a champ, like he takes everything, but he can't see a foot in front of his face clearly."

"So he really might be discharged?" Abraham asked.

"I'm afraid so," Frank replied. He picked a thin towel up from the washstand and twiddled with it as he spoke. "None of us boys want him to go. No one in the regiment dislikes him. He never rubs anyone wrong. He's so encouraging, and even when he was homesick, he kept our spirits up and gave us hope. I found the Lord because of him. He's been a blessing already. I hate that this happened to him. It was a fire at your farm, right?"

"Our aunt and uncle's farm, but yes," Reuben replied. "He saved our little brother from getting burned. That's how he got the burn on his leg."

"I'd wondered. He told us it was carelessness on his part. He didn't say what he was doing or how he got it." Frank shook his head and looked at the closed door.

"Do you mind if we wait here until the doctor's finished?" Rebecca asked after a moment of silence.

"Not at all." Frank turned to her and grinned. "Jonas has spoken highly of your entire family, but especially about you, Miss Rebecca, isn't it?"

Rebecca blushed and blinked quickly. Susan looked at her and smiled, and Reuben glanced up at Frank and winked. The soldier hid a chuckle.

He gathered his composure and added, "I'm not

sure how long the doctor will be with him. If you'd rather, the mercantile is next door. You can take a look around there if you'd like. I'll come fetch you once the doc's finished."

Rebecca turned to Reuben and said, "Let's do that, Reuben. I'd like to get acquainted with the mercantile anyway, since we'll be buying our items there from here on out."

"Right." Reuben offered his hands to her and Susan and helped them to their feet. "Thank you, Frank, for being so kind."

"Naw, don't mention it," he said, grinning. "Any friend of Jonas is a friend of mine."

# CHAPTER 22

# Whistling Creek

The Ross siblings exited the hotel quickly, avoiding the boy at the desk with care. They walked outside onto the porch, then took the stairs to the street. It was dusty, but the earth was packed in, making it easy to step on. They turned to their left and strolled next door to the mercantile. It was the only other two-story building in the town besides the hotel. They walked in, and Rebecca was hit in the face with a wave of homesickness. The inside of the mercantile was set up so similarly to the Wood Family General Store back home that it nearly brought tears to her eyes. A young girl with long black hair and blue eyes was working the counter, and for a moment Rebecca flashed back to Augusta, with Molly Wood smiling at her and asking if she could come over soon. Rebecca shook her head as the girl asked Reuben, "Can I help you four?"

Reuben seemed distracted, for he couldn't get his words out. He instead just smiled and motioned for Rebecca to speak.

"We're fine, thank you," she said. "We just came to look around. We just moved here and are waiting to visit a friend at the hotel."

"Well, then, welcome to Whistling Creek!" the girl said.

Rebecca looked around. "Whistling Creek?" she repeated. "Is that the name of this town?"

The girl laughed kindly. "You moved here and you don't even know the name of your town yet?"

"We haven't really been here that long," Rebecca replied, laughing along with the girl, who seemed about Susan's age.

The girl nodded sympathetically. "I understand. The first few weeks in a new home are always hectic. I'm Mary Winslow. My father owns this store."

"Nice to meet you, Mary. We're the Rosses. I'm Rebecca, and this is Reuben, Susan, and Abraham." Rebecca indicated each of her siblings as she said their names.

"A pleasure to meet you, Rosses. I—" Mary stopped as two little boys raced each other out of the back room of the store and nearly collided with Reuben, laughing loudly. "Georgie! Paul! I thought Mother told you not to run in the store when customers are in it!" she scolded the two, who were obviously her little brothers.

"Sorry, Mary," the oldest one squeaked, skidding to a halt. He couldn't have been more than six years of age.

She lost her tough front and said, "It's all right.

Run along and find Charles or Grace. Wasn't one of them supposed to be watching you two rascals?"

"Gracie *was* watching us," the oldest one answered, "but she—"

"Found a book," the youngest said, giggling.

Mary put her hands on her hips and shook her head in disapproval. "Of course she did."

A woman's voice from the living quarters of the building called through the open door, "Georgie! Paul! Where did you two run off to? You're meant to be helping me with the laundry."

The boys grimaced, and the littlest one made a face. Mary shooed them away with her hands and then turned back to the Ross siblings. "I'm so sorry," she said. "They haven't quite grown up yet."

"They were adorable," Rebecca replied, smiling at her.

"They're more like playful scoundrels when you're with them all the time," Mary quipped, reaching behind the counter and putting a length of fabric on it. She began to fold it.

"How many siblings do you have?" Reuben asked, finally finding his voice.

Mary looked up at him, her eyes twinkling. "I've got eight siblings. The oldest two are out of the house, so I'm the oldest at home. Is it just the four of you?"

"No, there are four younger ones back at the farm," Rebecca said, and Mary nodded in understanding.

"So you're the oldest sister, I assume. It's not an easy task, is it?"

Rebecca agreed, giggling.

"How old are you?" Susan asked in interest.

"I'll be seventeen on June twenty-third."

"Really?" Reuben exclaimed in surprise. "I'll turn seventeen the day before you!"

"For some reason I thought you were much older

than sixteen," Mary admitted. "You're much taller than my two older brothers were when they were seventeen. But then, my whole family is pretty short. I guess I should expect it." She said this last part dramatically, and the five laughed.

When they quieted, a customer stepped up to the counter and said, "Excuse me, Mary, but will you help me? I need a bolt of calico for Eliza's new church dress."

"Right away, Mrs. Chilton." Mary turned to the rolls of fabric hanging from the wall, but as she did so, she said to the Rosses, "It was lovely to meet you. Let me know if you need anything."

"She's a dear," Rebecca murmured as the four wandered through the store's offerings.

"So far," Abraham said, "the nice people are outnumbering the grouchy ones in this town."

"Thank *goodness*," Susan said, raising her eyebrows, and this sent them into laughter.

They didn't know why they were becoming so willing to laugh suddenly, although it was rather nice. Maybe it was because it was finally starting to feel like things were going their way and they were out of danger for the time being. Hopefully it stayed that way for a long time.

They continued to stroll around the store for the next ten minutes. Then, the bell above the door rang, and they heard Frank saying, "Rosses? The doctor's done with Jonas."

Frank was waiting at the front of the mercantile to escort them back to the hotel. They entered the hotel and quickly hurried up the stairs. Frank was the one who set this pace, and Rebecca thought she knew why.

"Are you trying to avoid the boy at the desk?" she asked quietly as they stood before the door to the soldiers' room.

Frank glanced at her and grinned. "You mean

Eric? Yeah. Our regiment has taken to calling him a drill sergeant. He's tough as nails. And just about as friendly too."

Reuben and Abraham looked at each other, fighting the urge to laugh again. Frank opened the door to the main room, where two other young soldiers sat on the two beds set against the walls of the room. They stood in respect as the four Ross siblings walked in.

"This is Laurence Hughes and Scott Paler," Frank said, introducing them to Jonas's roommates. Scott was tall and thin, taller than even Reuben, and had a wide mouth and shaggy mop of blond hair. His uniform was wrinkled, as if he'd slept in it all night. Laurence was the exact opposite. He matched Abraham and Rebecca in height but was built as sturdy as an ox with large biceps and a broad chest. His black hair was clean shaven, and his uniform looked as if it hadn't even been worn. Even Rebecca was impressed with how much ironing it must have taken to keep it perfectly pressed.

Reuben shook hands with both of them and introduced himself, Rebecca, Susan, and Abraham.

"A pleasure to meet you, sir," Laurence said in a clipped British accent.

"You're English," Reuben said in shock, and Laurence smiled.

"And you are not. Why you Americans are so surprised whenever you hear us speak is beyond me," Laurence said, shaking his head.

"I'm sorry, I didn't mean to be rude," Reuben stammered.

"Ignore Lorne, pal," Scott said. "Don't let his stuffy manners do you one over. He's one of the biggest jokesters in the regiment. He just uses the accent to his advantage. Just call us Scottie and Lorne. It's what our friends call us."

Laurence broke into a smile as he admitted, "It's

true. Apologies if I made you uncomfortable, old chap." He patted Reuben on the back.

"No harm done," Reuben assured him. "I have two younger brothers, and we always joke around, don't we, Abe?"

"Boy, do we," Abraham agreed.

"Can we go in and see Jonas now?" Rebecca asked, her eyes begging.

"Of course." Frank waved for the four to follow him into the adjoining room. Jonas lay on his back, facing the ceiling. A bandage was over his eyes. "You have company, Jonas," Frank said.

"Rebecca? Reuben?" he asked, starting to sit up.

The two eldest Ross siblings rushed to his side and kept him down.

"It's all right, Jonas, don't get up," Rebecca soothed. "We're here."

Jonas relaxed and laid his head on his pillow. "How's Emily? I assume she's feeling better, or else you wouldn't have both come."

"Her fever broke yesterday evening. She's tired, but she ate a little bit of breakfast this morning," Rebecca told him.

He smiled, then listened. "Is it just you and Reuben?" he asked. "I would think I would have heard Anna by now."

Reuben gave a chuckle. "Susan and Abe came with us, but we left the younger ones home. We didn't want to overwhelm you. Speaking of which, how are you doing?"

"Okay," Jonas said, shrugged. He motioned to the bandage across his eyes. "Doc Vendette is hopeful the salve he made will bring down the inflammation a bit and help me see again before my regiment leaves in a couple of days."

"Can you at least see more clearly than you could after the fire?" Abraham questioned.

"Nope," Jonas replied brightly. "They're still just

as bad, if not a little worse."

"Oh dear, Jonas," Rebecca whispered, brushing a curling wisp of hair from the soldier's forehead. "I'm so sorry."

"For what, Becca? You didn't start the fire." Jonas reached out, trying to find her hand. She noticed and placed it in his. He patted hers reassuringly. "It'll be all right in the end, I'm sure. Everything happens for a reason."

"You're an inspiration to us all, Jonas," Susan said gently from the foot of the bed.

"Aw, I don't know about that, Su. I have learned over time that it's best when something challenging happens to just accept it as God's plan. He always knows what's best for us. So why would I need to be mad or sad or stressed when He has it all in His hands?"

There was a sniffle from the doorway, and the four Rosses looked behind them to see Frank wiping at his eyes in embarrassment.

"Sorry," he said in a trembling voice. "I just . . . I just really needed to hear that. Phew, I'm sorry." He ran his hands over his face and then tried to smile. "It's been a hard two days."

Rebecca smiled back at him. "We know. We've had plenty of days like that. One minute you're all laughing, the next moment you're crying, and then laughing again. It's just called life. It's not easy."

"Boy, it sure isn't."

"We heard you may be discharged from the army," Abraham said to Jonas. "What are you going to do if you are?"

"I've been lying here all day asking myself the same question," Jonas replied, "and honestly, I haven't come up with an answer yet."

"You can't travel home if you can't see," Rebecca said. "The journey is already dangerous enough as it is."

"I know."

Frank stepped forward, his hand rubbing his chin as he suggested, "If you can't continue on with us, why don't you write to your parents and propose they settle in this town? It seems like a nice place, and you've already got friends here. Do you think they'd move out and stake a claim? So many are doing so."

Jonas raised one finger in the air. "I still hope I won't be discharged and can travel on with you boys, but if I am, once I'm allowed to use my eyes again, I could write them and ask. It's worth a try, at least. My father was considering moving somewhere west eventually. He has the western bug like most of our country."

Rebecca gasped and pressed her hands to her mouth. "Would that mean you would stay out here, and that your parents and Molly would join us here in Whistling Creek?"

Jonas laughed. "Of course, Becca, if they say yes! Would you mind if Michael Jones moved out here as well? Because—"

"No!" Rebecca said in excited disbelief. "He didn't!"

"He did," Jonas confirmed with a grin at Rebecca's delight. "At least, he should have. He told me before I left that he planned on asking Molly soon to marry him."

"Oh my goodness! I'm so happy for Molly! That's wonderful," Rebecca exclaimed, clapping her hands together.

"They were always perfect for each other," Susan said.

Jonas grinned. "Say, are you four hungry? Let's go downstairs to the kitchen and eat. It's nearly suppertime."

"You're on bed rest," Rebecca protested as Jonas sat up and swung his legs over the bed.

"I'm allowed to go downstairs and eat, Bec," Jonas told her as he undid the bandages around his eyes and wiped the salve from them with a towel.

Rebecca put her hands on her hips and looked at Frank for the truth. He nodded. "The doc did say Jonas could go downstairs for suppers only. He showed Scottie, Lorne, and me how to apply more salve and bandages once we're done eating."

Rebecca consented, and the Ross siblings joined the four soldiers in the dining room. It was a wonderful evening. They ate a delicious meal, told stories, and met many other soldiers in Jonas's regiment who all had something fond to say about him. No one wanted the night to end. Eventually, Rebecca, Reuben, Susan, and Abraham bade Jonas and their new friends good-bye and climbed onto their horses before riding away. As the sun began to set and they rode over the plains filled with dancing grass, Rebecca said, "That was the most fun I've had in such a long time."

"It certainly was," the other three agreed.

Rebecca patted Star's neck, and they eased into a gallop. Reuben saw this, and pressed Malachi to follow. Susan and Abraham looked at each other before urging Johnny and Sunny to go faster. They raced toward the farm, all laughing, and Reuben shouted, "I love Whistling Creek!"

# CHAPTER 23

# New Friends

"This is the land we chose," Reuben announced as he pulled on the reins to stop the horses.

Three weeks had passed since the doctor had come to take care of Emily. She was still slightly thin from her battle with the sickness, and today was the first day she had been allowed to leave Aunt Caralee's watchful eye to go on such a large outing. She was sitting in between Reuben and Rebecca on the wagon seat, with a quilt draped over her shoulders and one of Reuben's arms wrapped protectively around her.

Jonas's regiment had continued their trek,

departing on their set date. Rebecca, Reuben, Susan, and Abraham were sad to see Jonas's friend Frank leave, as they had built an immediate bond with the kind young man. They were happy, though, because although Frank, Laurence, and Scottie moved on, Jonas stayed. The salve had slightly improved his eyesight, but not to the point where his commander thought he would be useful. He had been discharged from the army and taken a job at the mercantile, since he had experience running the counter. He sent a letter to his family telling them about the change of plans and asking them if they wanted to join him in Whistling Creek. Jonas and the Rosses waited eagerly for their response.

The wagon stopped in a small clearing surrounded by a small forest. The trees were tall and sturdy, and Joshua was itching to get off Malachi and climb up a particularly tall maple tree.

"This place looks amazing, Reuben!" Abraham

shouted from atop Star.

Reuben grinned and jumped down from the wagon seat. He tied Kettie's and Johnny's halters to a tree and then ran over to help Joshua tie Malachi's reins to another.

"Where are you going to tie Susie?" Sarah asked, referring to Kettie's newly named foal. Sarah slid off the back of Malachi after Joshua and landed in the soft green grass. Susie was a very dark brown except for a white stripe that ran down the center of her face. She was already a favorite because she was very gentle.

"I'm not going to tie her anywhere, Sarah," Reuben replied, watching with a smile as Susie frisked around by her mother. "She'll stick close to Kettie because that's where the food is."

Sarah laughed. "That makes sense." She clapped her hands and coaxed, "Come here, Susie. Come here."

The foal tossed up her head and trotted over to Sarah, who was offering her a sugar cube from her apron pocket. Sarah giggled and gently rubbed Susie's white stripe. Susie nudged her in the stomach, asking for more treats, but Sarah shook her head and patted the foal's back.

Rebecca got down from the wagon with help from Reuben and then walked around the clearing where they would build their log cabin. "Trees," she whispered, clapping her hands in delight. "There are so many trees." She spoke more loudly so Reuben could hear. "It's just like Missouri. But . . . every place else we've passed has been so barren. How are there such gorgeous trees here and nowhere else?"

He grinned widely. "We are right next to the nearest river as well as a couple of creeks and springs. Trees shoot up here unlike in other areas. We have about . . . ten acres with trees, the acreage nearest to the water sources, and the remaining seventy acres are clear already. I thought you'd like this place to live because I know how much you miss the trees we had on our farm back home."

"It's lovely," Rebecca said softly.

"Where are Sam and Lydia going to live?" Joshua yelled from his seat on a branch in a large maple tree. He'd made a break for it as soon as he'd gotten off Malachi's saddle. He swung his legs back and forth, holding onto the limb above him.

"Well, the Homestead Act gave us one hundred and sixty acres of land, so Sam and I decided to split it. He has eighty acres on one side of the river, and we have eighty on the other side. That means we're only about a mile away from his place, because he also chose to build where there are more trees, just on the opposite side of the river. We'll probably end up building a small footbridge across it, once we get the cabins up," Reuben explained, looking at his brother with a sparkle in his eye.

Joshua grinned eagerly, knowing what his older brother had in mind. He waved Reuben up and patted the branch next to him. Reuben grabbed onto the branch closest to him and climbed up until he was sitting next to Joshua and looking out at the clearing.

"I'm going to call this tree Lookout Point," Joshua said, gazing out at the view.

The siblings on the ground waved to the brothers in the tree. Joshua made a silly face and giggled.

"Be careful up there!" Rebecca called, just the slightest amount of concern on her face.

Reuben gave her a thumbs-up. "Hey, I like that, Joshua! Let's name every part of our farm as we go along," he suggested.

"That's a great idea."

The two boys climbed down the tree and landed on the ground with hearty thuds. Anna danced around and laughed.

"We're finally west!" she sang. "We're finally west!"

Sarah laughed and grabbed her little sister's hands. "Yes! Yes, we are!" she cried in delight.

The two spun around, and Spottie, their little collie puppy, ran in and out of their legs, barking and yipping.

Emily kneeled and called, "Come here, Spottie!"

Spottie ran to Emily and licked her face. Emily fell backward, giggling and rubbing the pup.

"Spottie, down! Aw, yuck! I think his tongue got in my mouth," Emily said in disgust, wiping her face with her dress skirt.

Rebecca grimaced and suggested that Emily come rinse her mouth out with some water from the water bucket. Emily happily agreed.

"Okay, we need to start cutting down some trees so we can get to work on our cabin," Reuben announced.

"Oh, I hate that we have to," Rebecca mourned. "They're all so beautiful!"

"I know, but don't worry," Reuben said as he jogged past her, "we won't cut them all down. We will still have plenty once we're done."

He and Abraham climbed into the wagon and grabbed their axes.

Rebecca watched with a thoughtful frown. "It's going to take you two an awful long time to cut down enough trees to build a house—not to mention a barn as well," she said skeptically as she tied on a faded pink bonnet. "Should Susan and I help?"

"You can't swing an axe," Abraham said, a slight challenge in his tone. With a grunt he jumped out of the wagon and landed on the ground, the impact sending a shock through the heels of his feet.

Rebecca put her hands on her hips. "Oh, yes I can, Sir Abraham. If you don't remember, I helped

Pa and Reuben build our house in Missouri when I was only eleven years old, and I handled an axe as well as they did." Abraham arched his eyebrows in surprise. He'd forgotten all about that. Feeling that she had won the battle, Rebecca motioned to the trees and said, "So, Reuben, shall we?"

"No need, Becca. Mr. Johnson and his sons said they'd come over today and help," Reuben replied.

Susan's eyes lit up. "Really? All of them?"

"If you're meaning Judah," Abraham teased, "he couldn't come. He had other important business." He snorted to himself as he picked up his axe and slung it over his shoulder.

Susan rolled her eyes and looked at Reuben for a truthful answer.

"I think they're all coming, Susan. If you're so eager to do something, Becca, you could make a good meal over a fire for all the hungry workers you're going to have," Reuben said, knowing his sister would already do so without thinking twice.

She nodded and asked Susan and Sarah to help her. They went off in search of sticks to make a fire to cook over. Mr. Johnson and his five sons soon arrived in their work wagon armed with two-man saws. Another work wagon came behind theirs. It held four men, who introduced themselves as the Wilkensons. The father's name was James, and his three sons were David, who was sixteen, Daniel, who was fourteen, and Stephen, who was eleven.

"Welcome to the community, neighbors!" Mr. Wilkenson said as he clapped Reuben on the back. He explained that whenever a new family moved to town and needed a hand building a house, all the local families pitched in and helped.

Reuben thanked him heartily, and the men got to work.

The Wilkensons had also brought two-man saws, and all the young men paired up and chose a thick tree to cut down. Reuben was paired with Judah. The saw went back and forth on the trunk of the sturdy oak in a rhythm. Judah was a lot of fun to talk to and made the work feel like play. He had blond hair and the brightest blue eyes Reuben had ever seen. He had a slight build and was tall and limber.

"You sure are lucky to live in a place with loads of trees nearby," Judah said once as he pulled a grass spur out of his pant leg. "We weren't so lucky. We had to cut trees from three miles away and lug them to our house when we built it. You must have at least ten acres here of good, strong, mature trees. Reminds me of New York State."

"Does it really? I wouldn't know, seeing as how the farthest east I've been is Kentucky." Reuben, while Judah was talking, was trying to place Judah's accent. Ever since Abraham had pointed it out the day they met Judah at his family's farm, Reuben couldn't ignore it. He had to know what it was.

And just like Susan had said, he sometimes used words that Reuben didn't know—not bad ones, just different ones.

When Reuben asked Judah where he was originally from, he answered, "My family immigrated to America from Germany. That was eight years ago. We lived in New York State for about six years and have lived out here the rest." Judah chuckled at Reuben's astonished look. "If you think I have a bit of a German accent, you should hear my oldest brother and all my cousins. Since they lived there the longest—other than my parents—they have the strongest accents. All my family is fluent in German, though. Even my youngest siblings, Lillian and Hannah, who are ten, speak it fluently, though they've lived in America most of their lives, because we all speak it in the house."

Reuben mopped the sweat off his forehead with a

handkerchief. "That's amazing! Imagine being able to speak two languages. I'm still trying to perfect this one!"

Judah chuckled and flicked a spider off his pants. "I used to speak four," he added shyly. "German and English are my first languages, but I also learned to speak Polish and Dutch, because there were a lot of people from Holland and Poland where my family lived. I remember close to none of it now, but I used to know enough to carry on a decent conversation. 'How are you today?' in Polish is *Jak się dzisiaj masz?* In Dutch it's *Hoe gaat het met je vandaag?* That's about as much as I can say anymore."

Reuben's mouth dropped open. "That's even more amazing!"

Judah started to answer but was interrupted by his father, who rattled off something in German from three trees away.

Judah shrugged his shoulders, nodded, and

responded, "Yes, sir, Papa, I know. *Es tut mir leid, wir wurden abgelenkt.* Won't happen again." He then turned to an astonished Reuben and said, "See what I mean? Papa almost always speaks German to us, though he is nearly perfect at English."

"What'd he say?" Reuben asked in interest. "And what did you say in the middle of your sentence?"

Judah laughed. "Sorry, it's a bad habit. I said, '*Es tut mir leid, wir wurden abgelenkt*' or in English, 'I'm sorry, we were distracted,' and before that, he said, '*Hören Sie auf, Kontakte zu knüpfen und fangen Sie an zu sägen!*'"

Reuben's mouth was open. "What?"

Judah took up his side of the saw again as he translated, "Stop socializing and start sawing!"

# CHAPTER 24

# Building the Foundation

The work went quick with twelve people helping, and by the time Rebecca banged on a tin plate with a ladle to signal dinner being ready, the workers had already sawed down fifteen trees, about a quarter of what they would need to build a house. They had also built up quite the appetite. Rebecca had made bean porridge and added in some dried moose meat, roasted potatoes, and boiled carrots to give it more of a hearty substance. She had made a very large amount of it, so all the workers could have as much of it as they wanted. Everyone sat down on the ground with their bowls and merrily talked about their plans and swapped stories. Stephen Wilkenson and Joshua found a lot in common with each other and ended up doing more talking than they did eating. Meanwhile, the rest of the families caught up with the latest news from town and beyond. Susan wanted to know if Samuel and Lydia had help building their house.

Judah, who was sitting on the log next to her, replied, "Yes, they do. Two out of the four other farm families that live here went to help them out. We always make sure to *'helfen Sie den neuen Leuten,'* or help the new people, as it's said in English."

"I like how German sounds." Susan smiled bashfully at Judah, and he grinned back as he leaned forward to refill his porridge.

After dinner the men got back to work, and the girls helped when they could. Reuben called Susan over and asked if she would fetch a bucket of water from the nearby spring. He told her to follow the small footpath to it. She nodded and took up a metal bucket.

Susan walked down the narrow path to the spring. Soon the cleared land turned to a forest, and the shouts and yells of the men were replaced with a symphony of bird songs and animal calls. A warm summer breeze rustled through the treetops, adding to the beautiful melody of the forest. Instantly Susan knew she would love living here. The forest reminded her of the small grove that was at the edge of their old property in Missouri. After about a ten-minute walk, Susan heard the sound of bubbling water, and she knew she was getting close to the spring. She came in sight of it and caught her breath. A mother elk and her young baby were drinking from the spring. The baby was dark brown with a tannish underbelly, and its brown eyes glittered. The mother was a larger version of the baby and just as beautiful, if not more so, in an elegant way. They looked up at Susan, no fear in their eyes, but curiosity was present. The baby took a step forward, and Susan held out her hand. As the mother watched on without a hint of worry, the calf approached Susan and sniffed her apron with his wet, black nose. Susan stood stock still, smiling as wide as she possibly could. The calf snuffled her hand and looked up at her questioningly. Susan could barely believe this was happening to her. It was a dream come true to be so close to a harmless baby animal, and no one was there to witness it. She slowly reached out her hand and stroked the calf's soft, fuzzy back. He took a step backward, and Susan removed her hand. The calf seemed to smile at her before turning and trotting back to his mother's side. The two animals, after a moment's pause, loped into the foliage and were gone.

*Amazing,* Susan thought to herself as she bent down with the bucket and filled it with the cool spring water. *Absolutely amazing. How glad I am that we didn't turn back when I wanted to. I already love it here. It's beautiful.*

Susan finished with the bucket and walked back to the clearing. When she got there, she put a ladle in the bucket and walked to where the men were working. She brought it to Martin Johnson and Abraham first, then moved toward Judah and Reuben. She was within twenty feet of them when she heard a deafening crack.

She also heard Reuben yell, "Susan, look out!" and Judah shout in panic, "Susan!"

Susan didn't quite know what was going on. She looked up and saw a tall pine about to crash to the ground right above her. But before she even had time to scream, Reuben and Judah were there, and they pushed her out of the way of the falling tree.

*Susan looked up and saw a tall pine about to crash to the ground right above her.*

The wind was knocked out of her as she hit the earth, and Reuben ended up with his face in the dirt beside her. Judah went sprawling across the ground ten feet away.

There was chaos as everyone started shouting and yelling and running toward them.

"Are you three all right?" Mr. Wilkenson asked in concern.

"I-I'm fine," Susan answered, sitting up, even though her lungs were still stinging. She shook her head and blinked to regain her breath. "Reuben, are you all right?"

Reuben, whose face was still halfway in the dirt, replied with a muffled "Mmm hmm." He sat up, spit some dirt out of his mouth, and clarified, "I'm fine. Judah?"

"Never been better." He was already on his feet, feeling around for any injury. Judah's blue eyes were filled with relief. He offered his hand to Susan, then helped her up. "Glad you're all right," he said softly, with a gentle smile of assurance.

Susan let out a deep breath and nodded. "So am I." She gave a small laugh, which ended up as more of a sob as she thought about how close the tree had come to falling on her. Rebecca, who was standing nearby, heard the emotion and gave her sister a comforting hug. Rebecca felt Susan give a long sigh as she let her body relax in her older sister's arms.

"We're so sorry," Peter Johnson said as Susan dusted the dirt off her dress.

"We didn't see you walking in front of the tree we were working on," his brother, Walter, added. His face was bright white, and he looked close to tears.

"It's all right. I wasn't paying attention to where I was walking," Susan replied. "There's no harm done, really. Everyone's fine, so let's go with that." She picked up the bucket, which had fallen to the ground, spilling water everywhere and creating small mud puddles. She sighed. "Guess I'll have to get more water. Thank you, Reuben and Judah, for saving me."

Both boys nodded. "Of course," Reuben said, giving her shoulder a little shake.

Later in the afternoon, Mr. Johnson and Mr. Wilkenson continued sawing trees while the boys grabbed their axes and started to prepare the trees. First they chopped off the branches and then made a large notch at both ends of the tree. This was done so the logs would fit on top of each other without sliding off. Then the boys hacked the bark off the trees. Joshua helped with this part, and he was very proud to use his small axe alongside his older brothers and the others. After they had cut down and notched each tree, all the men helped plan out the house—with Rebecca overseeing it all, of course. In the dirt they used a shovel to draw the outline of the house. The main room would be about twelve feet long and about the same width. The second room, which would serve as the bedroom, would be about the same size as the other room. It would be tight, but they would eventually add on and make it bigger. Right now, the main concern was making a structure for them to work from in the near future.

The workers rolled the first logs in line with the small trench they had dug with the notches in the trees facing up. By then, the sun was beginning to set, so the Johnsons and the Wilkensons packed up and promised to be back early the next morning.

The Rosses wouldn't be going back to their uncle and aunt's house to sleep. Instead, they'd sleep in their covered wagon like they did when they were traveling. Reuben and Abraham took one mattress from the wagon and set it under the wagon, and Rebecca and Susan started to make supper in the cast-iron pot that hung over the fire by a spit. Abraham had made the spit earlier in the day by driving two forked sticks into the ground and resting another straight stick across the two forked ones.

Abraham and Joshua ran down to the spring with two buckets each. They hurried back to the clearing with full buckets and handed them off to Susan. She and Rebecca started to make creamed carrots to go alongside the dried moose meat Aunt Caralee had given them. Susan poured some of the water from one of the buckets into the cast-iron pot, and Rebecca cut some carrots into thin slices, then put them in the pot. The sisters chatted on various subjects, but it was mainly the prospect of having a real home soon that excited them the most. Meanwhile, the boys tended to their animals.

After twenty minutes, Reuben came over and asked, "Ready for me to get the fire going?"

Rebecca nodded. "Yes, please. Thank you, Reuben."

"Anytime, Becca."

# CHAPTER 25

# Danger in the Dark

Emily sat up in Lookout Point with a smile on her face. Joshua, Sarah, and Anna sat around her on the thick branches of the strong maple tree.

"I'm so glad you're all better, Em," Joshua said from the branch across from hers.

She grinned her mischievous grin. "I'm glad I'm all better too. You don't know how much I missed getting to play and climb and see you all!" Emily laughed and pulled herself a branch higher.

Lookout Point was about ten feet above the

ground on some of its lowest branches, and from it you could see all three acres of the clearing.

"Will you four come down?" Rebecca called to them, looking up from the pot of creamed carrots she was stirring. "It's time for supper. Careful, though!"

Joshua, Sarah, Emily, and Anna scrambled down from the tree and joined their four other siblings by the wagon.

"Isn't it nice to have just the eight of us here, all together?" Reuben asked as they ate their supper together by the hissing and crackling fire.

The siblings looked at each other and agreed. They hadn't been alone together since before joining up with Samuel and Lydia.

"I sure missed getting to be with just all of you," Rebecca said as she helped Anna cut the dried moose meat on her tin plate (Anna tended to send the meat and the plate flying). "I know it may sound a little bad, but I've just gotten used to being with my favorite people in the world."

"I have to agree," Abraham added. "I'm looking forward to living by ourselves again. It was way too crowded in Uncle Robert's house with fourteen of us in it! I felt like I was always getting stepped on."

There was a hearty buzz of agreement to this statement. The children continued with their meal, conversing on various subjects. Joshua was itching to know if he could have a round of target practice with Reuben's gun the next morning, to which Reuben said no, they were starting on the house as soon as the sun was up, and he needed his help. Rebecca and Susan were discussing what colors the drapes in their new house should be—Rebecca wanted red and Susan wanted blue. And Abraham was teasing the younger girls about a ghost in the woods he called Old Smiley. The legend—which Abraham made up—was that a ghost roamed their woods, looking for people to smile at. The tale was funny and not a bit scary, and Anna found herself wishing Old Smiley would show up. She wanted to show him her smile now that she had lost her first bottom tooth. When she asked, Abraham promised to take her on a hunt to find Old Smiley once their house was finished.

After supper, the conversations and stories continued as Reuben pulled out his guitar and played a few tunes under the moonlight.

When he paused in his playing, Sarah said, "I can't believe we're finally making Pa's dream come true. It feels like such a long time ago since we decided to follow after it."

Everyone softly murmured things along the lines of "Yes, it does" and "It's amazing we made it."

Just then, something growled outside the clearing, causing the siblings to jump to their feet.

"What was that?" Anna asked, her blue eyes

huge, bumping into Susan as she backed up. Susan took her protectively into her arms and held her close.

"I have no idea," Reuben answered, springing for his shotgun which sat on the ground. He quickly loaded it and took the safety off. Then he spoke with a grave severity in his voice that scared Sarah and Emily. "Don't any of you get in front of me, no matter what. I'd die if I accidently hit one of you should I have to use my gun."

Rebecca nodded and drew a small pistol from her apron pocket while putting her one arm out as a barrier for the children. The siblings stood in a group nervously, whipping back and forth as they heard branches snap on one side, then a second later a growl on the other. Joshua and Sarah gripped each other tightly, holding on so their knuckles turned white. There was a rustling of leaves, and then suddenly three wolves came into the light of the fire.

The children cried out in panic. Abraham grabbed his brand-new gun from where it was lying against a rock and aimed it at them, though his hands were shaking so badly he'd surely miss his target.

"Stay back!" Reuben shouted at the wolves in a strong voice. Pointing his gun into the night sky, he quickly said, "Becca, Abe, on my count, fire into the air to scare them off. Ready? One, two, three!"

The younger siblings covered their ears as three gunshots rang out. The wolves cowered but didn't run away like Reuben had hoped. They had strength in numbers, and they could sense the fear in the family.

"What do we do now?" Susan asked, hiding Emily and Sarah behind her skirts and tightening her hold on Anna.

The wolves growled, and Spottie growled back. Emily screamed, and Anna cried out in fear. The spirited puppy, though only three months old, was ready to defend his owners, and his little tail straightened in the air threateningly. Reuben's eyes widened at their pet's bravery—and foolishness—and he instructed, "Sarah, pick up Spottie *now*."

She quickly obeyed and scooped the pup into her arms, softly telling him to be silent.

Reuben's brain was scrambling to find an idea. Out of the corner of his eye, he saw Lookout Point not twenty feet away from the siblings. A plan formed in his head.

"Okay, I've got an idea," he said as Abraham picked up a huge branch and waved it at the wolves in warning. "Everyone, slowly back up and then climb up Lookout Point. I'll keep the wolves back." He kept his voice low and calm as not to give away that they were scared. But he knew the wolves could sense their fear, despite his bluffing.

"But what about you?" Rebecca asked in panic as the wolves got closer. "That won't work anyhow.

They've made a half circle around us! No, no, no! Shoo! We're not your prey! Scat! Get out of here!" Rebecca placed herself protectively in front of Susan, Sarah, Emily, and Anna, and Joshua guarded their back. Abraham was sweating profusely, glancing at his older brother, willing him to get them out of trouble.

Reuben bit his lip and looked around wildly. He spotted a few big nuts sitting on the ground next to the fire. Remembering back to what had happened when the prairie fire burned the nuts, another idea came to mind. He bent down and collected a handful of them, hoping that his slow movement would not spark the wolves to attack.

"Everyone, cover your face and turn away from the fire!" he warned as he threw the nuts into the fire. Susan quickly turned and sheltered the other girls with her body, and Rebecca covered Anna. Abraham had a hard time obeying, wanting to know what Reuben was doing. He whipped around as soon as he saw what his brother had thrown in, blocking his face and shielding Joshua.

The nuts exploded with the heat, making the fire hiss and flash and crack. The girls screamed. Reuben picked up more and chucked them into the fire. It sounded like a Fourth of July celebration with hundreds of firecrackers rocketing off. The last nut to hit the fire shot back and hit Reuben in the arm. He winced, but he was aware of the wolves whimpering and cowering into the shadows.

Abraham took charge as he twisted around and started throwing rocks and shouting at the wolves. The other children followed his lead. The wolves turned and ran into the forest, tails between their legs. They preferred easy prey, not prey that fought back!

"Thank the Lord!" Rebecca cried, gathering Anna and Emily in a tight hug once the predators were far out of sight.

Susan and Sarah let out hiccupping laughs, and Abraham took a deep breath and let it out with a whoosh as he wiped the perspiration off his forehead.

"What did you throw in the fire, Reuben?" Joshua asked, waving his hand in an effort to clear some of the smoke away.

Reuben was rubbing his shoulder as he replied, "Just some nuts that I noticed explode easily when put in fire." He grimaced and bit his lip.

Rebecca's brow creased in concern. "Are you all right, Reuben?" she asked as she slid her pistol back into her apron pocket.

His answer was without hesitation, and he stopped massaging his shoulder. "I'm fine."

"Are you sure, Reuben?" Susan questioned. "You look like you're hurt."

Reuben winked at her. "I'm sure I'll be fine.

The last nut I threw exploded and hit me in the shoulder. No serious problem. I'll be right as rain tomorrow. You'll see. Believe me, Becca. Don't look so worried. Honest, I'm fine. I'd tell you if I wasn't, now, wouldn't I? Besides, I wouldn't be able to hold my head up around here if I knew I'd been injured by a nut!"

Rebecca smiled at him and nodded. She knew he would be up front with her if he really was hurt, or else he would have signaled that he was but didn't want to concern the others. She could tell from his eyes that he was fine. Reuben said he'd had enough music for one night and was going to bed. As he walked back to the wagon, his seven siblings stared after him.

"Will he be okay?" Anna asked in a whisper as Susan set her down.

"I'm sure he's fine," Rebecca answered. "He knows when he's hurt." She sighed. "Though I must admit, I am still a bit shaken from that wolf encounter." She paused. "Let's get to bed."

Everyone agreed and walked to the wagon. The siblings changed into their nightclothes and rubbed some salt across their teeth to clean them. Joshua and Abraham climbed under the quilt on the mattress they shared with Reuben under the wagon and told him good night.

"Night, you two."

Up in the wagon, the girls climbed into their beds and snuggled deep into their pillows, with Spottie sleeping curled up on the little girls' bed. Soon the only sounds in the clearing were the occasional hoot of an owl, the scurrying feet of field mice, a howl of a wolf, and the peaceful deep breathing of the Ross family.

# CHAPTER 26

# Finally Home

True to their word, the Johnsons and Wilkensons were back and ready to work as soon as the sun rose. The children, who had been up for quite some time, were ready to help, and Reuben's shoulder was perfectly fine, as he had predicted.

Right away, they started to work. Joshua, Abraham, Edward Johnson, and Stephen Wilkenson were assigned to finish notching and preparing the logs. The four other Johnson boys helped Reuben, Mr. Johnson, Mr. Wilkenson, and his two other sons stack the prepared logs on top of each other. It took a while, but before dinner the men had the walls about five feet high.

Dinner was more dried moose meat and some roasted potatoes.

"Now, how about some music before we start working again?" Mr. Wilkenson proposed, brushing some potato from his beard.

"Great idea, Father!" Daniel applauded.

Reuben ran to get his guitar, and the Wilkenson boys ran to their wagon. David came back with a fiddle, and Daniel brought a harmonica. The three struck up a rollicking tune.

Judah jumped up and asked Susan if she knew how to two-step.

"I do," she bashfully responded as Judah helped her to her feet.

Joshua and Sarah also jumped up and tried to follow along to Judah and Susan's steps. Abraham and Rebecca stood up and joined the dance. Anna grabbed Stephen's hands, and he laughed and

danced in tiny, bent-over circles with her. Everyone
else clapped to the beat. Susan and Judah were
by far the best partners on the dance floor, but if
Reuben and Rebecca had been paired, no one could
have beaten them. The two were amazing to watch
when they danced together. The three musicians
played four more songs on their instruments, which
the pairs also danced to. All too soon the music
stopped, and the men stood up and said they needed
to get back to work. The dancers slowed, gasping for
breath and smiling at each other.

Judah bowed to Susan. "You're the best dance
partner I've ever had," he said courteously. "Just
don't tell my four sisters!" he added in a playful
whisper. "They might get *beleidigt*, or offended!" He
winked.

Susan laughed and blushed a soft pink. "Thank
you, Judah. It was a lot of fun."

He smiled and nodded, then ran to start working

again.

From a distance, Rebecca had watched the exchange with a thoughtful expression, and now she smirked as Susan approached. "That Judah Johnson sure is something, *isn't* he?" Rebecca said.

Susan looked at her sister and giggled. "Oh, Becca, no!" Her blue eyes were sparkling.

Rebecca winked and squeezed her sister's shoulder.

The men continued to add layers to the walls, and the girls started to gather together materials for chinking. The three oldest Ross girls and Joshua hurried down to the spring with some large wooden buckets and filled them with mud, leaves, and sticks from around the spring. The siblings came back to the clearing with full buckets. Anna's mouth dropped open when she saw her siblings' mud-streaked clothes.

"You went and played in mud and didn't tell

me?" she asked in disbelief.

Rebecca chuckled as she placed her bucket down by the side of the cabin. "No, Anna. We got mud for chinking."

"What's chinking?" Anna questioned in fascination.

Rebecca motioned for Anna to come see what she was doing. "Well," Rebecca started, pulling some mud from the bucket beside her and filling a crack in between the log layers, "chinking is when we take a thick, muddy paste and fill the gaps that are left when logs are laid on top of each other. It helps to keep the house insulated and keeps the bugs out."

Anna shrugged. "Okay, neat. I'm gonna go play with Emily. Bye, Becca!"

Rebecca chuckled and continued to smear mud all over the cracks.

"You've got some mud on your nose," Joshua told Rebecca.

She turned and smirked at him mischievously. In the blink of an eye, she reached down to the chinking bucket beside her on the ground and plopped the mud onto her little brother's nose.

He squealed in surprise. "Becca! You put mud on my nose!" Joshua wiped it off with his shirt sleeve. "Why'd you do that? I mean, other than you just being a silly big sister," he said as he continued to fill the cracks in the walls.

Rebecca smiled and answered, "Well, Joshua, in a way it's a lesson. No matter what you look like—or if you have mud on your nose—we'll always love you for who you are. Now here, take my handkerchief and clean it off all the way."

Joshua wiped his face, then handed the handkerchief back to her. "Thanks, Becca."

"For the handkerchief?"

"For the lesson."

"Of course, little brother. Now, let's get back to

301

work."

When the time came for the Johnsons and Wilkensons to return home to their farms, the walls of the Rosses' home were nearly seven feet tall. All the children were very excited because tonight they would sleep in their house for the very first time. Abraham and Reuben pulled the white canvas off the wagon and climbed onto the logs at the top of the wall. They stretched the canvas over the room that they would be sleeping in and secured the canvas with some wooden hooks Abraham had made earlier in the day. Then Reuben and Abraham brought the straw tick mattress into the room. Rebecca brought a quilt from the wagon, and Reuben used his hammer to drive some thick wooden pegs through the quilt and into the front door frame.

"This'll put a barrier between us and the wolves, bears, mountain lions . . ." Reuben trailed off when he saw Joshua's face turn pale. He jerked his jaw in embarrassment for scaring his little brother. "Nothing to worry about," he added reassuringly.

Joshua nodded. "Nothing to worry about," he repeated confidently. He moved the quilt aside for Abraham and Rebecca, who were carrying one of the children's trunks into the house. Reuben saw them and ran to the wagon, climbed in, and then hopped out with the children's other trunk in his arms. Joshua moved aside the quilt for him as well.

Out on her picket line, Bessie mooed contentedly and settled in for the night. Abraham peeked out the hole for the window and asked Reuben if he should check the area Bessie was at to make sure there was no grass that would make her sick.

Reuben shook his head. "I already checked the area around Bessie's picket line, and it's fine as far as I can tell."

Susan called to everyone saying supper was ready.

As they sat down in the grass outside their new house, Susan apologized for making the same meal twice.

Reuben chuckled and said, "You don't have to apologize, Susan. Your cooking is the absolute best . . . I mean, besides Becca's, of course." He shot a teasing grin at his sister.

She brushed off the jest with a wave of her hand and a roll of her eyes.

"I think Rebecca's is the best too," Susan said humbly. "She cooks so much faster than I do."

"Oh, Susan, you're both the best!" Reuben laughed out loud and pushed his straw hat to the back of his head.

"I love our new house," Anna remarked sometime later. She stretched out on the grass, then quickly sat up. "Ew! More fire ants!" She stood up and shook her dress and her hands. "Are they gone?" she asked with a whimper.

Rebecca looked her little sister over. There were no fire ants as far as she could tell, and she told Anna this. Anna sighed in relief, then moved to the safety of Abraham's lap.

Soon the sky went from a red-orange to a dark blue-gray as the sun set behind the distant mountains. The siblings sat in the grass quietly. Anna and Emily were playing with their dolls, and Sarah helped Rebecca and Susan clean the dishes. Susan cleaned the dishes in a bucket filled with soapy water; then Rebecca rinsed them off with water from another bucket filled with water; and lastly, Sarah dried them with an old towel and set them in their crate.

Reuben pulled out his guitar and picked out a few soft tunes. Anna returned to her seat on Abraham's lap, tucked her head into his neck, and closed her eyes sleepily. Abraham was her favorite person in the world, and everyone knew it. Abraham put his arm around the tired girl and leaned against the cabin wall.

"Ready to go to bed?" Rebecca questioned as she helped Sarah lug the crate of dishes into the wagon.

Reuben nodded and pointed at Anna, who was now sound asleep in Abraham's arms.

Rebecca chuckled and said, "All right then. Let's go into the house—oh, my, it's been so long since I've said that! This is a dream come true."

Abraham carefully stood up and carried Anna into the house, then laid her on the straw tick mattress next to Spottie. Anna sleepily reached out and patted the pup, who yawned and stretched. Reuben held the quilt aside as the siblings entered the cabin. The patchwork quilt soon hung limp as Reuben, too, passed through the door into his new house.

# CHAPTER 27

# Bear Claw Grove

Around four o'clock in the morning, the rain started. It made popping sounds against the white wagon canvas that served as a makeshift roof. It wasn't specifically an annoying sound, but it was loud enough to wake the people sleeping under it.

Reuben woke up bleary-eyed, and for a moment his brain told him he was in the wagon, just outside of Independence, Missouri. His confused brain then looked around and thought, *If this is the wagon, it's bigger than it was last night.* Then he got his bearings and sat up in bed. His movement awoke Abraham and Joshua, who both yawned and sat up beside

Reuben.

"What time is it?" Joshua groaned, rubbing his eyes.

"I don't know, but hush, you'll wake the girls," Reuben whispered back.

"Well, I'm still tired and I'm going back to bed," Abraham said, lying back down. "You boys going to join me?"

Reuben nodded, then realized how silly of an action that was, seeing as how it was quite dark in the room and no one could see his head nod. He lay back down beside Abraham and inhaled deeply. The smell of rain was strong, and the *pop, pop, pop,* of the droplets against the wagon canvas was soothing. Reuben smiled to himself, then took hold of Joshua's nightshirt and pulled him to his back on the bed. The boys chuckled and started to drift off when they heard a different sound. A sound of something snuffling around. Snuffling . . . *in the house.*

"Do you guys hear that?" Joshua asked hesitantly, pulling the quilt up to his neck.

"Yes," the two older brothers answered nervously.

Reuben and Abraham sat up and looked around the room. They could see the outline of things, just not in detail. There was the trunk, the two other beds, and what was that other shape in the room? Reuben and Abraham both spotted something on all fours coming toward them.

"Do you see that?" Abraham asked, his voice cracking.

"Uh huh," Reuben replied, swallowing hard.

In the middle of the bed, they could feel Joshua shaking. Reuben put a hand on Joshua, then gave a small shout as the creature jumped onto the bed.

"Spottie!" the boys cried together in relief as the pup started licking Abraham's face.

In the other beds, the five girls sat up.

"What's going on?" Emily asked sleepily.

"What time is it?" Anna added in a grumpy tone. She hated being woken up.

"And why'd you boys yell?" Rebecca said, getting out of bed to light a lantern.

When the soft glow of the lamp filled the room, Reuben, Abraham, and Joshua looked at each other and burst out laughing. Through their laughter, Reuben explained to the girls that they had thought they heard something and scared each other by doing so, but it was only Spottie. They'd been so tired, they'd forgotten all about him being in the house. Once Reuben was finished, all the girls were laughing along with them.

"What happened to being the brave protectors?" Susan teased, pinning up her hair.

Reuben put his hands up in defense. "Look, it was dark out," he said, trying to make an excuse.

Abraham snorted, and it set them laughing again. Finally, everyone stifled their giggles enough to get dressed into their day clothes.

"Let's get an early start on those chores," Reuben suggested to his brothers.

They tromped out the door, and Sarah hurried after them to feed the chickens and collect their eggs. Reuben handed Abraham and Joshua some feed sacks for the six horses: Malachi, Star, Kettie, Johnny, Sunny, and Daisy. Susie, Kettie's foal, would happily nibble on some feed but mostly drank her mother's milk. Reuben then gave Sarah a metal bucket with the chickens' feed in it. The sun was not fully up yet, and a thick fog covered the forest like a mother bird's wings that cover her chicks.

The chickens, who had roosted in Lookout Point for the night, flew down as soon as Sarah called, "Here, chicks! Feeding time!" She tossed the feed to them in small handfuls.

The Rosses' ten chickens flocked around Sarah, greedily gobbling up the mixed grains. All of the chickens had names and personalities to fit. There was Omelet—Abraham had named this one—Betty, Belle, Solomon the rooster, Red, Matilda, Big Ma, Dolly, Breakfast—another name by Abraham—and Coco. Coco was Sarah's favorite because she was so sweet, calm, and predictable. Red was her least favorite. He was the junior rooster in the group and the meanest chicken to walk the face of the globe. Every time Sarah or any of the siblings came near him, he squawked and threatened to peck their feet. Sarah just tried to keep her distance and let Red be Red.

Soon the bucket of feed was empty, and Sarah went on a hunt to find any eggs the chickens might have laid. She looked behind a bush and found one there, then checked next to Lookout Point and discovered two. She found five more in some other random places as well. With the eggs sitting carefully in her metal bucket, Sarah walked into the house and handed them off to Rebecca. She nodded to Sarah and set the bucket on the floor of the main room. The dirt floor had turned to mud because of the rainstorm, and now the hems of Rebecca and Susan's skirts, which brushed the ground, were caked with mud.

The girls went to look for some dry sticks to make a fire with. They walked into the forest and hunted around trees, in bushes, under logs, and next to rocks for dry branches. The five came back with their arms full of sticks. Under the spit in the main room, they built a fire, which they were able to do since they didn't have a roof yet. Susan made hasty pudding for breakfast and spooned it into eight blue-and-white china bowls.

Watching Susan, Anna asked, "Su, if we call our good plates and bowls 'china,' in China do they call their good things 'America'?"

Susan laughed as she handed a bowl to her

youngest sister. "I don't know, Anna. Maybe they do, and then again, maybe they don't."

"If *I* were in China," Anna said, drawing out the *I* as she kicked her legs and looked around, "I would call my plates America."

"I'm sure you would, Anna." Susan smiled, wiped her hands on her apron, and stirred the hasty pudding.

"Rebecca!" Reuben's shout carried into the house.

She looked up from the tea that she was warming over the fire and called back, "I'll be there in a minute."

"Becca, hurry!" he yelled again.

"Emily, can you run outside and tell the boys it's time to eat?" Susan asked, trading her already dirty apron for a clean one.

Emily nodded and ran out the door. The scene that met her eyes made her screech. Reuben,

*Reuben, Abraham, and Joshua were as high up as they could go in Lookout Point.*

Abraham, and Joshua were as high up as they could go in Lookout Point, and a huge bear was clawing at its trunk. That's why Reuben had yelled for Rebecca! Reuben broke a branch off of Lookout Point and swung it at the bear as a warning if it started up the tree. Reuben spotted Emily and shouted, "Tell Becca to get the gun! Hurry, Emily, hurry!"

Emily sprinted inside and cried, "Becca! Becca! Bear! Bear—and Abe, Reuben, Joshua!"

Poor Emily was so scared she could hardly make sense of her sentence. But Rebecca had understood enough. She ran out of the house with a plate and ladle in hand, and Susan followed with a pot and a metal spoon. Sarah, Emily, and Anna realized what they were doing and quickly grabbed a pan and a spoon or plate for themselves. They rushed outside and started banging on their pots and pans as loudly as they could, shouting, "Get out of here! Shoo!"

Reuben, Abraham, and Joshua joined their

shouting, and Joshua pulled branches from the tree and threw them at the bear.

The noise and the branches annoyed the bear so much that, with a snort, he dropped on all fours and lumbered back into the forest.

"Are you boys all right?" Rebecca asked as they climbed down from Lookout Point.

Leaping lightly to the ground, Reuben reached up to help Joshua down before saying, "We're fine. That bear just snuck up on us, is all. We all got up in the tree before he got to us. And I've come up with a name for the clearing our house is in."

"What is it?" Sarah asked.

"Bear Claw Grove."

The siblings all burst out laughing.

# CHAPTER 28

# A Joust in the Kitchen

"Becca! We're up in the sky!" Abraham exclaimed as he sat atop the log wall of their cabin.

It was Monday afternoon, three days after the bear encounter. After taking Sunday off, the Johnsons and Wilkensons had arrived early in the morning, ready to finish building the fireplace and put the roof on. The fireplace would be used to heat the home and cook their food. Once they got the roof on, there would be a "barn dancing," even though they didn't have a barn yet. Susan was especially looking forward to the barn dancing, because Judah Johnson had already asked if she'd be his partner. She'd shyly accepted and now eagerly awaited the dance. The Rosses had invited the two other farm families and their cousins, aunt and uncle, and of course Jonas Wood to come and celebrate. The women of these families would come bringing what Mr. Wilkenson described as "a whole mess of food."

As Abraham and Reuben waved to the six siblings who were staring up at them with smiles on their faces, everyone felt a glimmer of excitement.

"We've just about got the roof done," Reuben shouted down. "We're going to be able to have the dance tonight!"

The children cheered happily.

The sky was a beautiful blue, and a couple puffy white clouds floated lazily by. A soft breeze was blowing, rustling peacefully through the trees.

Putting the roof on was hard work, but it went quick with eleven men working on it. Within no time, the house was done. The freshly cut logs made it smell wonderfully, and the inside was clean and dry. There was a small porch on the outside and, at Rebecca's request, a large window in the main room so that light and the breeze could stream in. There was no glass in it, but the men attached shutters so she could close them at night or in bad weather.

Judah came and stood by Susan as the men put the last log into place.

Susan spoke first. "You boys have done an amazing job building the house. Without your help, we'd probably still be cutting trees. Thank you, Judah."

He smiled. "It's fun to help new friends—or *'neue freunde,'* as we would say in my first language."

Susan looked thoughtful. "So, that's German for new friends? Noy fronds?"

Judah laughed. "Close! It's *'neue freunde.'* Try it. It really is not that *schwierig*—difficult."

"Noy . . . fronds?" Susan started, then turned red in embarrassment. "Oh dear! I said it the same way as last time! Well, thanks for trying to teach me. I'm afraid I probably won't be very good at German."

Judah leaned against a tree as he replied, "It was wonderful for a first try, Susan. It's not an easy language, but neither is English. I'll have you speaking German yet. I know you can do it. Here, let's start with a simple good day this time, all right?"

"All right. I'll try again," Susan agreed shyly.

Judah nodded. "Great. Good day is: *'guten tag.'* It's simple enough. Try saying it. *Guten* is spelled exactly how it sounds, and *tag* is spelled like your game called tag but said differently, more like frog with a *t* instead of the *f* and *r*."

Susan listened to him demonstrate once more, then tried. "Gu-ten tag. Guten tag! I did it!"

Judah grinned. "Yes, you did it wonderfully! Now, I must be going, so I'll teach you a quick good-bye. It's '*auf wiedersehen.*'"

Susan's eyes were wide by the time he finished. Judah noticed and said encouragingly, "Don't worry. You don't have to say it if you don't want. I'll teach you some easier words when we come back later this afternoon."

Susan smiled. "All right, Judah. Thank you again. I'm looking forward to being your partner."

"As am I, Susan," Judah replied, his blue eyes sparkling. "*Auf wiedersehen.*" He tipped his felt hat to Susan, then hurried to get in his father's wagon.

As soon as the work was done, the Johnsons and Wilkensons left to get freshened up and pick up the rest of their families. They had invited many other families as well, and the Winslows, who lived in town, offered to give Jonas a ride.

As soon as they'd left, the Ross children hurried

to unpack and arrange what little possessions they'd brought from Augusta. They swept the floor; then everyone rushed to get cleaned up.

As Sarah washed her face and Susan did her hair, Sarah said, "You like Judah, don't you?"

Susan seemed to be in her own world as she pulled a pin out of her hair, allowing it to fall to her lower back. She blinked, then grinned. "Who, me? No, I don't . . . I mean . . . he's just—really nice. He's a *'freunde,'* is all."

Sarah looked at her older sister with a raised eyebrow. "A what? Did he teach you German?"

"Well, literally a word or two anyway. That means friend."

"That's pretty neat," Sarah said, placing the washcloth on the basin's rim.

Susan nodded as she combed her part smooth. She braided her hair into one long braid and then pinned it into a low bun. "How does it look?" she asked Sarah, spinning around to show her sister.

Sarah grinned. "It looks great, Susan. I love how it looks with your deep blue church dress."

Susan curtsied, fingering the smooth material as she did so. "Thank you, Sarah. This was my favorite dress Ma ever made. It feels so elegant. I love the lace on the cuffs, the lace on the neck, and the row of white buttons down the back. I never get to wear it, so it feels so special. And . . . it makes me feel just a little closer to Ma every time I wear it."

Sarah smirked slyly at her sister. "Well, Judah is going to think you look gorgeous."

"Sarah!" Susan turned back to the mirror to fix a loose strand of hair, shaking her head at her cheeky sister.

"What? I'm serious. It's fun to have someone to tease! It's every sister's job to tease her other sisters."

"Then tease Rebecca about Jonas," Susan replied, as she moved behind Sarah to help her braid her hair. "Don't you notice how shy she gets when he's around? And how that pink color comes into her cheeks when she talks about him?"

"Just like how that pink comes onto *your* cheeks when you talk about Judah?"

"Oh, stop it, Sarah. I'm too young to even think about any of that stuff, and you know it. He's just been nice these past few days, and since I don't really have any friends here yet, well, he's just been friendly to me. But," she added, looking at Sarah pointedly, "I am looking forward to meeting some other girls my age tonight. End of conversation?"

"Yeah, okay. End of conversation." Sarah grinned at her sister and smoothed out her dress. It was dark green, with sleeves that stopped just below her elbows. The dress was the longest she owned; her two others stopped just above her ankles, but this one was like all of Rebecca and Susan's dresses with a hem that reached the floor.

Emily bounced out of the bedroom, her shoulder-length auburn hair free with a blue bow in the back that matched her dress. The dress highlighted her dark brown eyes, and with her hair down instead of in a single braid like usual, she looked much older than six and a half.

Anna followed, tugging at the collar of her light pink dress and complaining to Susan that it was too tight. A small pink bow was in her chin-length hair, and once Susan loosened the collar, Anna's frown turned into a grin.

The other girls caught their breath when Rebecca came out of the room. Her hair was in her usual chignon bun with a couple strands of brown hair hanging loose. She wore her best dress, which was a deep violet. It reached to her ankles and pinched at the waist. The sleeves reached her wrists and had white cuffs.

"Becca, you look amazing," Sarah said softly, as

her sister walked over to the fire and pulled a pot of soup from the spit.

Rebecca blushed modestly. "Thank you, Sarah. It was Ma's old dress." Turning back into her practical self, she said, "Now, hurry. The boys are going to be ready in a minute, and people should start arriving anytime now."

The girls continued fixing each other's hair and smoothing out wrinkles in their dresses, but when Reuben, Abraham, and Joshua came out of the bedroom, they paused in surprise.

Reuben was as dressed up as the younger girls had ever seen him. Instead of his usual straw hat, plain shirt, suspenders, and brown pants, he wore a felt hat, a light blue shirt with a dark brown vest, and pants of the same color. Abraham was dressed the same, except his shirt was light green. Joshua, on the other hand, wore his best white shirt, suspenders, and dark brown pants. He never liked hats, but he had made an effort this time and put on one of Abraham's old felt hats. His cheeks had been scrubbed to a rosy red.

"You boys look wonderful," Rebecca complimented. "Joshua, I think that hat looks very nice on you."

He grinned sheepishly. "Thanks. I guess I sort of like it."

Reuben walked up to Rebecca and made a deep bow. "Fine madam, will you do me the honor of being my partner at the dance?" he asked with a British accent.

Rebecca laughed and nodded. "Absolutely, kind sir. I thank you for your invitation."

This sent the siblings into a fit of laughter. They never were that proper, not even Rebecca and Reuben!

"What are we all, royalty?" Abraham chortled and bowed with a flourish of his hand, mocking

Reuben.

"Indeed we are, Duke Abraham Wallace," Rebecca replied, curtsying as she pulled out Abraham's dreaded middle name.

"Okay, if I'm Duke Abraham Wallace," he quickly shot back, "then you all are . . . Queen Rebecca Martha, King Reuben Joel, Duchess Susan Harmony, Lady Sarah Faith, Sir Joshua Edwin, Princess Emily Jane, and Princess Anna Pearl."

"Hey, I'm a princess!" Anna squeaked, grabbing Emily's hand, and the two pretended to greet their adoring subjects.

"My Lady Sarah," Joshua said in a voice much deeper than his usual, "will you please me in so much as to accompany me on this lovely evening in England? We are going to attend a ball in the king and queen's castle."

"Oh, indeed, Sir Joshua. I would be delighted to join you!" Sarah said, taking his outstretched arm and snickering. "But hark! Your armor is dirty. What a disgrace to Their Majesties!"

"What? Really?" Joshua lost his proper tone, looking anxiously at his shirt. Had he gotten dirt on it? Sarah's laughter told him she was teasing. Straightening and broadening his shoulders, Joshua cleared his throat and said solemnly, "Ah, well, that is a disgrace, my lady. I shall have to jump into the sea to clean it! Far be it from me to show up dirty to a royal celebration."

Sarah sniffed and attempted to look haughty, but a grin snuck its way in.

"I wouldn't go to that party if I were you, Sir Joshua," Abraham warned, leaning in close to the knight-in-not-so-shining-armor and dropping his voice to a loud whisper.

Joshua rubbed his chin, pretending to be scholarly. "Oh? Pray tell why."

Abraham's eyes were sparkling, but his tone was

serious. "Never would I spread a lie, but rumor has it that the king is a great big ugly troll!"

"Oh, a great big ugly troll, huh? You just started a war, Duke," Reuben said, grabbing a broom from Susan's hands. He held it out and advanced toward his brother. "On guard!"

Abraham whipped around, and when he turned back, he was wielding a deadly metal ladle with the handle facing "King" Reuben. *"Touché!"*

They started hitting each other's weapons viciously, with the girls and Joshua rooting them on. The two blocked and parried and struck light blows at their opponents.

"Never start a war with the king of the castle!" Reuben cried, swinging the broom so hard it made Abraham backpedal three paces.

He leapt forward and exclaimed, "Ah, but do not underestimate the power of a little brother!" He stopped, coughed awkwardly, and corrected himself.

*"Touché!"*

"I meant duke. Do not underestimate the power of a duke! I am fighting for the honor of dukes everywhere who don't like their middle names! Take that, and that! And—oh, gotcha there, your kingliness!"

Someone knocked on the door of the cabin, making the battle abruptly come to a halt as the boys scrambled to put away their things.

"This isn't over, Duke Wallace," Reuben whispered in his ear as Rebecca went to open the door.

"Indeed it is not so, King Joel," Abraham replied with a wink, jabbing his brother in the ribs. Reuben jerked and responded with his own jab at Abraham's side.

"Just put a truce on it for a night's time, ye royal bickerers," Rebecca said with authority, standing by the door. A prim expression grew on her face as she folded her arms across her chest. "As High Queen, I decree a hold on the Battle of Wing and Duck for a full twelve hours."

Abraham's mouth fell open, aghast. "Did you hear that, King Reuben? She has openly insulted us, and in front of a crowd of dignitaries as well! Wing and Duck indeed! It's King and Duke, Miss Queen!"

Rebecca flitted a hand in his direction, acting disinterested. "No, it is Wing and Duck, and I shall hear no further argument."

The brothers looked at each other, contemplating a joint revolt, but another loud knock sounded on the door, and they sighed, then swept their hats off and bowed on one knee in respect.

"Yes, Your Highness," they said in unison.

Rebecca rolled her eyes with a chuckle as she undid the lock.

# CHAPTER 29

# Rebecca's New Partner

The door opened to reveal Uncle Robert, Aunt Caralee, and Lizzy waiting eagerly on its threshold.

"Lizzy!" Sarah exclaimed.

"Sarah!"

The two cousins ran to each other and gave each other a hug as the rest of the siblings welcomed their first guests.

"This is going to be *so* much fun!" Lizzy said as Rebecca walked out with Aunt Caralee to help her bring in the food she'd brought for the dance. They came back in carrying a roasted turkey on a platter and a bowl of mashed potatoes. Joshua's eyes lit up when he saw it. He *loved* any type of food, especially the kinds he didn't get to have very often.

"Have you ever been to a dance before?" Sarah asked.

Lizzy nodded. "Yes, we had one when we finished building our house. Ma made me wear my best dress. Do you like it? It used to be hers." She spun around to show Sarah. It was a faded pink with a rose print. The length was down to her ankles, and the sleeves were long.

"It's great, Lizzy! It looks really good with your red hair up in that bun! But I thought you couldn't wear your hair up yet. I'm not allowed to put mine up until I turn fourteen."

Lizzy grinned. "This is my very first time wearing it up. You know I just turned fourteen a week ago." She spun around again, finishing in a pose with her right arm arching over her head and her left hovering around her waist.

"That's right! Do you like it?"

Lizzy shrugged and touched her hand to her hair. "Well, it's not as comfortable as I thought it would be, but it sure does look pretty."

Sarah and Lizzy sat down in a corner of the main room and traded stories. Sarah told Lizzy how the older boys had just declared a "war" among each other, and in turn, Lizzy told her how Lydia had just discovered she and Samuel were expecting their second child. They laughed and giggled as they whispered and visited.

"The Johnsons are here," Rebecca announced a few minutes later.

Susan's eyes sparkled in excitement. She hurried to greet them, and the rest of the families followed. Mr. and Mrs. Johnson and their five sons and four daughters were climbing out of their wagon by the time everyone made it outside.

Judah Johnson walked over to Susan and said, "Hello, Susan. You look very *wunderschönen* tonight. That dress looks very nice on you."

"Thank you, Judah . . . what does that mean?"

"It means beautiful."

Susan blushed. "Oh, and guten tag to you too."

"Very good, Susan! See, I knew you could do it. Now, come over here. I want you to meet my sisters. I've been telling them all about you. I get what it's like to be shy, especially in a new place, so I hope you find friends in my siblings." Judah led her over to the four girls, whom Mr. Johnson was about to introduce.

There was nineteen-year-old Alice, sixteen-year-old Elise, and the twins, Lillian and Hannah, who were ten. All of them had blond hair and blue eyes like their brothers, and Alice had a very strong German accent that matched beautifully with her gentle smile. When she talked, sometimes a German word slipped in, and she would quickly correct herself. It seemed she wanted to speak that most of the time and only speak English when she had to, unlike Judah, who had an amazing ability to switch from speaking English with Reuben to saying a sentence in German to his brother.

"We've brought lots of food," Alice told Rebecca, her eyes glittering. "And I think it will all be gone before the night is over, because my brothers have *very* large appetites. *'Große Esser,'* we say in German. Big eaters."

Both giggled.

"Who is going to be your partner for the dance?" Rebecca then asked.

"My brother, Martin. Elise is going to dance with Edward, and Lillian and Hannah with Peter and Walter. I'm surprised Judah is, uh, dancing with a *mädchen*, a girl. He's rather *schüchtern*—uh, shy, I mean—and normally only dances with us. Who will you be dancing with?"

"My brother, Reuben. Only . . . oh! I don't think I'll be able to, now that I think about it. He'll be playing his guitar, I guess. He's so gifted at it, and I know all my siblings will want him playing it. Neither of us thought of that," Rebecca said. She looked at the ground to hide her disappointment.

"Oh. I'm sorry."

There was a pause; then Rebecca shrugged. "It's all right. I'm pretty tired anyhow. I don't think I could dance if I wanted to."

"Who are the rest of your siblings *tanzen*—dancing—with?" Alice asked sweetly. She sat down on a stump, and Rebecca did the same.

"Well," Rebecca started, "you know who Susan's dancing with. Abraham, who is the same age as Edward, usually dances with Susan, but I don't think he'll be dancing at all tonight, except for maybe a tiny spin or two with Emily and Anna. Joshua and Sarah always dance together. They're cute to watch, because Joshua isn't a very good dancer. They trip every once in a while."

"That is *niedlich*—or adorable. Sorry, I think in German and then try to speak in English. Sometimes I don't switch fast enough." Alice blushed and looked at her feet.

"It's all right, Alice. I think it's beautiful."

Another wagon rumbled up, followed by four others. The first one held the Wilkensons: Mr. and Mrs. Wilkenson and David, Daniel, and Stephen, along with Marianne, who was right in between David and Daniel in age. In the second wagon came another farm family who introduced themselves as the Winch family. There were Mr. and Mrs. Winch and their two children. In the third wagon arrived a new farm family who said they were the Honeycuts. There were seven in their family. Getting out of the fourth wagon were Mr. and Mrs. Winslow and their seven children. Jonas Wood came with them, having caught a ride from town. The bandages were off his eyes, and he seemed able to see a slight amount better than before.

"Hello, Ross family!" he said as he grinned. He was wearing an outfit like Reuben's. He lifted his hat to Rebecca, and she waved, then walked over to him.

"How are your eyes?" she asked.

He blinked them quickly. "They don't burn as much anymore, and I can see a little better, the best since the fire."

Rebecca crossed her arms suspiciously. "How much better?"

"Well," Jonas said, squinting his eyes into focus, "you're wearing a purple dress, for one, and it has lace on the cuffs. And you have your hair in its usual bun."

"It sounds like you've definitely improved since

the fire," Rebecca said.

"To be truthful, Reuben told me what you're wearing."

Rebecca gasped, and Jonas laughed long and loud. "I'm joking! I'm joking! Honest! I haven't even talked to Reuben tonight."

Rebecca playfully shoved his shoulder, and he smirked.

"You and Reuben dancing together like always?" Jonas asked, and Rebecca's smile wilted.

"No. He's playing his guitar. I'll just watch everyone dance," she said softly.

Jonas hesitated, then rubbed the back of his neck and offered, "I'd be glad to be your partner, Becca, if you'll have me, that is. I think I can see enough to dance. Close up, everything is a whole lot clearer. The distance is still giving me trouble, but you don't need to see a long way to dance."

Rebecca's eyes lit up. "I'd love to be your partner,

Jonas! Thank you so much for asking!"

He grinned and, after excusing himself, walked over to Reuben and Judah to chat.

The last wagon came at that moment, carrying Samuel, Lydia, and Lilly. Samuel's fiery red hair was neatly combed, and he wore his best shirt, suspenders, and pants. Lydia's shiny black hair was pinned into a knot on the top of her head, and she wore a sky-blue dress that matched her smiling eyes.

"This is going to be so much fun! Who are you going to dance with, Becca?" Lydia asked as she carried a bowl of green beans into the house.

Rebecca, who was behind her bringing in a large bowl of stewed beets that the Honeycuts had brought, answered casually, "I'm dancing with Jonas Wood."

"Really?" Lydia questioned with a twinkle in her eye as she set the bowl of beans on the roughly made table that Reuben had built a few days earlier. He would make a better one in due time.

Rebecca recognized the twinkle and said quickly with a flush to her cheeks, "He just offered to be my partner because I told him Reuben couldn't be since he'll be playing his guitar. That's all. He was just . . . being a good friend."

Lydia slowly nodded. "I see."

Rebecca caught her cousin in a hug and exclaimed, "I heard Lizzy tell Sarah the exciting news! Congratulations on your new baby!"

Lydia broke into a huge grin. "Thank you, Rebecca! Lilly and Lizzy haven't stopped talking about it all week! I hope it will be a girl, for Lilly's sake, but of course Sam is *dying* to have a boy."

"I'm sure he is. When is it due?"

"Sometime in winter of next year, I think." Lydia rubbed her hands together in anticipation.

"Oh my!" Rebecca said. "That really isn't too far away! Oh, Lydia, how amazing! Have you decided on a name?"

Lydia nodded. "If it's another girl, we're going to name her Evelyn, after my mother, but if it's a boy, we'll name him Mark."

"After Sam's brother," Rebecca quietly finished, hugging Lydia tight.

The two shared a smile, then went to help the Winch family bring in their platters of food. By the time they were finished unloading all the food and desserts from the wagons, the table and the mattresses in the bedroom were full. There was turkey, fried chicken, smoked venison, and fried fish for meat; mashed potatoes, green beans, creamed carrots, stewed beets, baked beans, and cornbread for sides; and for dessert, three kinds of pie, a large batch of molasses cookies, and Mrs. Winslow had brought homemade donuts, something the Ross children had never tasted. Everyone couldn't wait to eat.

# CHAPTER 30

# A Fun Filled Evening

Joshua, Stephen Wilkenson, and Jonathan Winslow sat high up in Lookout Point, watching everyone else from a bird's-eye view.

"I wish we lived on a farm," Jonathan said dreamily.

"You mean you don't?" Joshua asked, pulling himself a branch higher.

Jonathan shook his head. "No. I live above the general store. My father owns the store. It's pretty tight upstairs. Three of my brothers and I share a tiny bedroom and two beds. It was *really* tight when my other two brothers, who are married now, lived with us. My three sisters share a small bedroom as well."

"Are you the youngest?" Stephen asked. He reached up and took a better hold on the branch above him.

Jonathan sat down on a branch and swung his legs back and forth thoughtfully. "Nope. I'm nine, but Minnie, George, and Paul are all younger than I am. They're eight, six, and four. My oldest brother lives in California now, and my second oldest brother, Oliver, lives in town with his wife. Now the oldest at home is Mary. She's seventeen."

Joshua bounced up and down on his branch while keeping a tight hold on the branch above him. "I've got seven siblings. Rebecca is the oldest, and she just turned eighteen in April. My oldest brother Reuben turned seventeen a couple of weeks ago."

Aunt Caralee called up to the three in the tree, "You boys come down from there; it's time to eat!"

"Oh boy!" Joshua, Stephen, and Jonathan cried, scrambling down from Lookout Point as fast as they could without falling.

"Did a bear really corner you in this tree?" Stephen asked as he landed on the ground with a thud.

Joshua nodded as his feet touched the grass. "Yup. But the girls scared him away. Now I'm so hungry I could *eat* a bear! Wait till you try Rebecca's blueberry pie! It's amazing."

Once the boys were out of the tree and the others were gathered up from their various conversations, Uncle Robert asked the blessing, and then everyone went into the house to fill their plates with more than they could eat. Once everyone filled their plates, they went out and sat in the field next to the house. The adults sat together while the children broke into smaller groups and sat in miniature circles. Sarah sat next to Lillian and Hannah Johnson, Minnie Winslow, and Caroline Honeycut, who was the same age as Sarah.

"Have you ever been to a dance before?" Lillian asked as she cut into a piece of turkey.

"I have," Caroline replied sweetly. "When our house was raised, we had a dance. Only the Wilkensons and Winslows lived here at the time, so it was a very small dance, but it was still very fun. I've been to a few others as well, including yours, Lillian."

"Oh, that's right!" Lillian said, then took a bite of mashed potatoes.

"What about you, Sarah?" Hannah asked quietly. "Have you ever been to a barn dance?"

Sarah shook her head, then frowned and nodded. "I guess so. Reuben said we had one when we built our house in Missouri, but I was two and I don't remember. I'm going to dance with my twin, Joshua. Who are the rest of you dancing with?"

"I'm dancing with my brother Jonathan," Minnie said, fluffing her dark brown dress.

"It's Walter—or Walt as we call him—for me," Lillian added.

"My brother Peter," Hannah said, pushing her blond braids behind her back.

"I'm dancing with my brother too. His name is Phillip. He's thirteen. This is going to be loads of fun!" Caroline exclaimed, nearly upsetting the plate on her lap. She lunged forward and caught it, picking up her bread roll from the ground and dusting it off.

"What was it like in Germany?" Sarah asked Lillian and Hannah after a few moments of silence.

Lillian, who was the more talkative of the twins, laughed. "Well, we were only two when we moved to America, so we really don't remember. If you come over to our house, you could get a small feel of what it's like, though. We all speak German to each other most of the time. Mama, Papa, Alice, and Martin speak it the most. And Mama makes the absolute *best* pretzels."

"That's really neat," Minnie said, tucking her shoes under her dress. "My family came over to America a few generations ago, from France. My family moved out here over five years ago. We were the first family here out of everyone in the entire town. It was lonesome."

"My family was the third family to move here," Caroline added, setting her plate on the ground. "We're coming up on five years. It's hard to remember living anywhere other than here anymore, but we used to live in Connecticut. My family came from England over a hundred years ago. My great-grandfather, Theodore, fought in the Revolutionary War."

"Wow," Sarah said with a smile. "My great-grandfather, Edwin, on my pa's side, fought in the Revolutionary War and served under George Washington. And my grandfather, Jeremiah, was in the War of 1812. That's where he met my grandmother. I think my family came over to America at about the same time as yours, Caroline. I'm not exactly sure where we came from . . . but I think my great-grandparents on my pa's side were Dutch. And I heard something about my ma having relatives in . . . I think it was Scotland and Ireland. Maybe. I'm not sure. My sister Rebecca would know."

"Our families are from all different parts of Europe," Lillian pointed out, looking around at the small circle of girls.

"It's true," Sarah said, nodding, "but my pa always used to say we became something even better when we all came here. We became Americans. And look, we're all from different countries, but here, together, we're a part of the same country."

"The country people come to for freedom," Caroline said, wiping her hands on her apron.

"The country people die for," Minnie added, looking down, "like my uncle Adoniram."

"And my cousin Mark," Sarah said, touching Minnie's arm comfortingly.

"We have something special here," Hannah whispered, smiling tentatively at her newfound friends. "Something worth dying for and protecting. A nation built on God and freedom. There's none like it in the world."

"The United States of America," Sarah said, staring off into the distance as she thought about the war taking place as they spoke. "And I can only hope we unite once again."

Joshua and Abraham were sitting with Stephen and Daniel Wilkenson, Edward Johnson, Jonathan

Winslow, and Phillip and Leonard Honeycut. Joshua was in the middle of telling the wolf attack story to Jonathan when Reuben, Samuel, and David Wilkenson jumped onto stumps, picked up their instruments, and started to play a well-known folk song. Between the guitar, banjo, and fiddle, it was a perfect sound. All the partners got together and began to dance.

Jonas walked over from his group of friends, held out his hand to Rebecca, and when she took it, he pulled her off her seat on the ground.

"Shall we dance?" he asked with a grin. He offered his arm to her.

"Yes," she replied, taking his arm and letting him lead her in the jig.

The yard became a rainbow flood of colorful bonnets, shirts, hats, and skirts. A young man, who was a part of the Winch family by the name of Andrew, jumped onto a tree stump and shouted out

instructions according to the music. It seemed most of the people were experienced dancers, following along to the orders with ease. *Most* people, that is.

"Oh, Joshua!" Sarah screeched as the twins tried to follow in the older children's and grown-ups' steps. "You just stepped on my foot—*again!*"

Joshua winced for her. "Sorry, Sarah. I'm not the best dancer."

Sarah backed up a little bit as Joshua's larger boot almost clobbered her small shoe for the third time. "Just be careful."

"I'm trying." He grinned and studied his feet, being as cautious as he could.

Susan and Judah glided around the field, spinning and dipping. Both were smiling shyly at each other when they bumped into Mr. and Mrs. Winch with a surprised "Oh!"

Both couples ended up on the ground in a heap. Judah jumped up and then helped Susan to her feet.

"Are you all right?" he asked frantically, his cheeks flushed in embarrassment. *"Ich kann nicht glauben, dass ich das gerade getan habe.* Oh, Susan, *Ich bin der tollpatschigste Mensch der Welt!"* He was so mortified he didn't even translate his frantic stuttering.

"Judah, what did you say? I don't speak German, remember?" Susan brushed herself off and looked up at him expectantly.

He swallowed and tried to smile. He seemed embarrassed he had rattled off in German. "It doesn't really matter. But if you must know, I said I can't believe I just did that. I'm the clumsiest person in the world."

Susan smiled at his sheepishness and assured him it was fine, then asked if Mr. and Mrs. Winch were all right. They stood up and brushed off.

"It's quite fine, Judah and Susan. No harm done. And what's a dance without one or two falls?" Mr. Winch said with a laugh.

Judah and Susan looked at each other for a moment, then Judah bowed, and they took back to the busy dance floor.

# CHAPTER 31

# We Did It

Everyone danced long into the night. About an hour after the sun set and the stars came out, the music finally slowed and the visiting families collected their empty platters and bowls and said good-bye to the Rosses.

Right before he jumped into the Winslow's wagon, Jonas walked over to Rebecca and said, "I enjoyed being your partner tonight, Becca. You're a wonderful dancer—don't tell Molly, but you're better than she is. She never could dance very well."

Rebecca laughed softly and the same pink color that had been on her cheeks when Jonas had asked her to dance crept back. "It was so much fun, Jonas. You are a wonderful dancer yourself."

He grinned at her. "Thank you kindly. I'll see you around, Rebecca," Jonas said, nodding.

"All right. Have you said good-bye to Reuben and the others?" Rebecca looked over at her siblings. Reuben was talking with Samuel and Uncle Robert, Susan was chatting with Judah and Elise Johnson, and Sarah and Caroline Honeycut were engaged in a lively conversation with lots of giggling involved. The rest of the siblings were playing tag with the other farm children.

"Yes, I've already said good-bye to them all," Jonas replied. "Now I better get going. I think I just heard Mr. Winslow whistle for his family to get in the wagon. I'd hate to keep them waiting, since they were nice enough to give me a ride. Well, it's been a pleasure, Rebecca. I'm so glad we're all together again. It feels just like old times, doesn't it?"

Although his feet had stopped dancing long before, his eyes continued to, and Rebecca loved how they danced.

She tucked a strand of hair behind her ear and gazed up at him shyly. "Yes, it certainly has. I'm glad you are going to stay out here for now. It's like a bit of home came with us."

"It certainly feels that way. Who knew God could use a moving regiment, a wildfire, and blurry eyes to keep us in the same town? Best friends all together again. I'll see you soon." With one more nod to Rebecca and another flash of his handsome grin, he hurried over to the wagon and climbed in.

"Good-bye, Jonas," Rebecca whispered softly, watching him go.

Over in the field a ways, Elise, Judah, and Susan were conversing when there was a sharp whistle from the other side of the yard. "That's Papa's call, Judah," Elise said in the middle of her brother's sentence.

His face fell. "Already? It seems like we just got here," Judah responded, smiling at Susan.

She shyly grinned back. "Well, it was lots of fun to have you all over. Elise, it was so nice to meet you!"

"It was *guten* to meet you as well," Elise said with a twinkle in her blue eye.

Throughout their conversation, Elise and Judah had slipped in bits of German, making Susan try to figure out what they said. Susan took a guess. "Um, nice?"

Elise laughed softly. "Close, Susan. It means good."

Susan smirked. "So, you're saying it was a *guten* guess!" She paused, then snapped her fingers, eyes glowing. "Oh, like *'guten tag,'* like good day!"

Judah looked at her in admiration. "Nice job, Susan. Well, Elise, I think it's time we should be getting on, since Papa called."

"You're right, Judah. *Auf wiedersehen*, Susan."

Susan raised her eyebrow thoughtfully and looked at Judah. "I still can't say that, and Judah's been trying to teach me to say it all evening. How about I say a good old-fashioned English good-bye. Not as pretty, but certainly easier."

The corners of Judah's mouth curved into a smile. "It's just as pretty, Susan, right, Elise?"

"Absolutely. Good-bye, Susan."

"Good-bye, Elise, Judah."

"*Auf wiedersehen*, Susan," Judah softly said, tipping his hat to her, and he and Elise turned and walked to their wagon.

Susan waved, then walked over to talk with Marianne Wilkenson.

Over in the bigger part of the field, nearly all the children were playing a rowdy game of tag. Joshua, Charles, Grace, and Jonathan Winslow were it, and together they dashed after the others. The friends ran around in circles, tripping over each other and laughing. The chasers could not successfully tag any of their opponents, so Charles Winslow waved for his brother, sister, and Joshua to huddle up.

"We can't catch them," he whispered, breathing hard with his hands on his knees. "We need a new plan."

"What if—no, that won't work." Grace shot down her own idea with a shake of her head.

"I've got no clue," Jonathan added with a shrug.

"How about we all go after the same person?" Joshua suggested under his breath.

Charles jerked toward him, eyes sparkling. "Say that again?"

"What if we all chase the same person, you know, gang up on them?" Joshua repeated.

"I like it," Charles said slowly, rubbing his chin. He and Grace were fourteen, and one could easily tell they were twins. Both had dark brown hair and gray eyes that were slightly too large for their face and a little upturned nose, along with a generous helping of freckles. "Let's all go after Stephen Wilkenson. He's one of the faster ones, and it will help our team if we can tag him and make him a chaser. Grace and I will come at him from his left and right, and Jonathan, you come from in front of him. Then, Joshua, you sneak up and tackle him from behind."

The teammates nodded and broke apart, pretending to go different ways and then suddenly turning on the youngest Wilkenson. Grace and Charles ran at him from different angles, and Jonathan sprinted toward him from the front. Joshua hid behind a stump, then launched forward as Charles shouted, "Now!"

"Whoa! Hey, I've got to go, that's my pa calling for us to get in the wagon," Stephen Wilkenson said just as Joshua lunged and tagged him on the shoulder, and the two tumbled to the ground in a tangle of arms and legs.

"No fooling?" Joshua asked skeptically with his hands on his hips and a suspicious smirk on his face as he rose, covered in bits of leaves.

"Honest—no fooling. I've got to get going," Stephen assured him.

"Oh. Okay then. I'll see you around. Hey! Maybe you can come over the day after tomorrow and we can play together! Ask your ma, okay? My sister Rebecca would be fine with it."

Stephen nodded. "I promise I'll at least ask. It would be so much fun. Now, I really must get going so I'll—"

"Hey, Joshua!" Charles hollered from the other side of the field. "You going to help us? We need to regroup!"

Joshua chuckled. "I'm coming! Bye, Stephen."

"Bye!" Stephen jogged over to the Wilkenson's wagon along with David, Daniel, and Marianne.

Joshua waved and then turned on his heel and resumed the wild game of tag. The Winslows were called to leave, and so new taggers had to be elected. This started a great debate that lasted nearly the remainder of the night, as almost everyone had already been it and those left were too young to really call it fair.

Sarah and Caroline hugged each other tightly when the time came for the Honeycuts to leave. They had learned they had much in common and were perfect friends. Soon, the Winch family left as well, shortly followed by both Willoughby families. After the company left, the Ross children sat on their new front porch and listened to the crickets sing. Reuben pulled out his guitar and lightly played and hummed some well-known songs.

"It's such a peaceful night." Rebecca sighed

contentedly.

Reuben stopped for a minute and smiled proudly at his siblings. "We've come a long way to get to this point. I know it was a lot harder than we expected, from tornadoes and bears— "

"To mountain lions and raging rivers," Sarah added, patting Spottie on the head.

"And wolves and lost horses," Emily chimed in.

"And low food and a wagon crash," Susan remembered softly, tucking her feet under her dress.

"And that virus that four of us got," Abraham said, pushing his straw hat to the back of his head. Anna claimed his lap as her seat, and he chuckled.

"What about the prairie fire?" Anna asked.

"Yes, and poor Jonas's eyes," Rebecca said quietly.

"Don't forget the strange fever Emily had and the tree that nearly fell on Susan," Joshua reminded his siblings.

Susan shuddered.

"And the wolves that I think wanted to make us their late-night snack," Rebecca said with a shudder, though she smiled.

"And the bear that cornered the boys in Lookout Point!" Anna said squeakily.

Everyone laughed, and Spottie yipped.

Reuben stood and opened the door to their new house. "Well," he said, lifting Emily onto his back, "even though it was hard and scary and we thought that we might not make it, look! We've finally made Pa's dream come true!"

Abraham pumped his fist into the air, and the others cheered.

Rebecca smiled at the bittersweet moment and hugged Joshua around the shoulders. As Emily tiredly buried her head in Reuben's back, and Anna did the same in Abraham's arms, Rebecca looked around at her siblings and softly repeated, "We've finally made Pa's dream come true, but you know what? I think that the adventure is just about to get started."

"With new friends," Susan said, walking through the door.

"And old friends," Sarah chimed in, thinking of Jonas with a smile.

"And new adventures," Rebecca added, following her sister. "It's more than I could have ever dreamed."

Reuben smiled at the siblings and said, "I agree, Becca. I have a feeling the real adventure is just getting started."

Abraham stood carefully to his feet with Anna in his arms. Joshua tugged on Abraham's shirt and said, "You know when the adventure starts?"

Abraham looked down at his brother with a grin. "When?"

"Right now."

Abraham chuckled as Anna grumbled in her sleep. "Why now?"

Joshua stuck his hands in his pockets and said sheepishly, "Because we've gotta go catch Star. She's loose from her picket line again."

Abraham looked at the horse, who was running through the clearing, enjoying herself to the fullest, and groaned. He looked at Reuben, who said, "She won't go too far. She'll be back by feeding time."

Abraham glanced down at Joshua and said, "No, the adventure starts tomorrow when we catch that crazy horse. For now, it's bedtime."

Joshua nodded. "Sounds good."

From inside the house, Rebecca called, "You boys coming in?"

"Yes, we are," Reuben said with a sweep of his arm. "We're coming in, because we're finally home!"

As Abraham and Joshua walked inside, Reuben tilted his face up toward the starry night sky and said in a whisper, "We did it, Ma and Pa." Tears built in his eyes, but he blinked them away.

He knew they'd be proud.

# The Journey
# Continues...

Made in the USA
Columbia, SC
12 May 2024

35208555R00207